WE THREE

Part One of TRIUMVIRATE

A Novel by John O'Connor

© 2008 by John O'Connor
All Rights Reserved.

ISBN: 978-0-6151-9499-8

What You Now Hold

This is an experiment. I wrote a novel called "Triumvirate" over the course of four years (finishing it just before my daughter was born). Numerous publishers and agents have declined it over the past seven years. I might have known that a novel written in homage to the E.R. Eddisons and Robert E. Howards of the world would be of limited commercial appeal. Rather than let it moulder in my hard drive (and in a number of hard copies in my closet) I have resolved in this new year to help it find its audience. Since the old world path of queries to agents and slush pile submissions has not succeeded, I am choosing the path of the new information economy.

Thus Lulu.com, thus this first experimental volume (which consists of the introduction and the first part of the novel). If you like it, there is more.

I hope you won't mind the rough-hewn nature of the map. I made it myself.

I hope you enjoy.

John O'Connor

January 2, 2008

For Ingrid and Megan, in love and gratitude.

Map: The Land of Thane

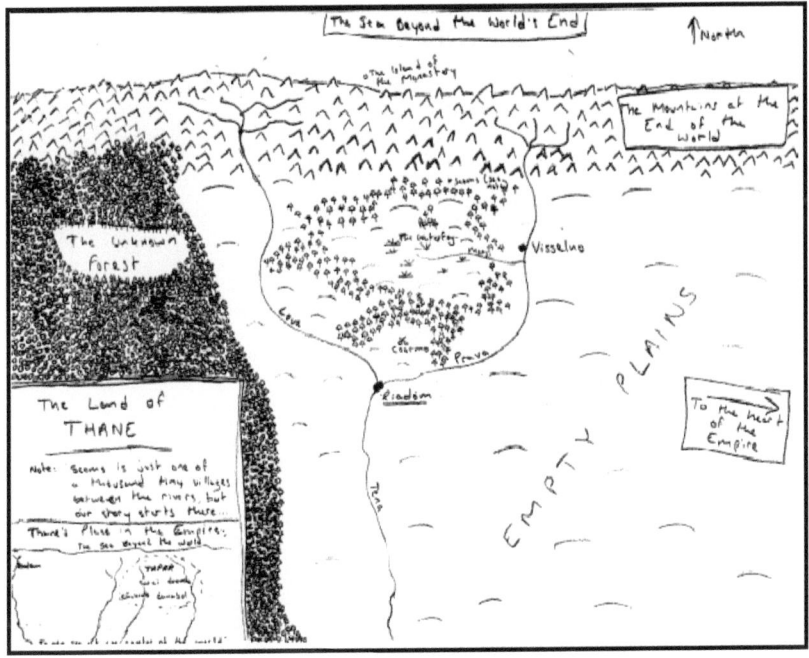

Prologue: True Belief

In the spring of the year before the year Zero, a new priest came from Riadom to the village of Scoms, which lay within faint sight of the mountains at the end of the world. He had traveled by barge up the wide river Prava, and from the port at Visselno he had ridden by oxcart into the mountain district, of which Scoms was one of the chief towns, and then through the forests and fields to what he had imagined would be a place of some consequence. It was hardly that. A sturdy fort sat on a middling hill that overlooked the wheat and potato fields, and from the fort a muddy road ran into the cluster of wooden buildings that made up the town. Thin columns of smoke trailed up from chimneys and cooking fires, and in every direction broad fields ran out from the town, ending at the line where the forests took up. From there, to the north, lay the mountains.

This region was known as the mountain district, but in truth the mountains had hardly begun at Scoms. A great range of peaks extended north from here to an unknown end, where some said that the land dropped off to nothingness and a man may look down on an endless field of swirling clouds. Beneath the clouds some said a cold sea roiled on forever northward into infinity. The mountains were the uncharted domain of bandits and land-toilers who had escaped from the fields what they might call freedom. It seemed to the priest that they had escaped nothing; their ends could only be cold and destitute amid the snows. To the south, where the foothills trailed off and the land rolled in vast and gentle waves, the grasslands and farming fields were fed by the two great rivers, Leva and Prava, which met far to the south at Riadom, the city from which the priest had set out some weeks before, the ancient capital of the land of Thane. This tiny and remote province of the great empire had at its center a great marsh called the Waterfog, and all across the land a mass of poor land-toilers farmed rocky fields under the watch of their betters.

The priest was a man of patience, as he had properly been raised to be in the seminaries and the schools, and he had not hurried to his new post in this distant and unfamiliar place. Anyone who met him knew his profession by sight. His slight build betrayed years bent over books instead of working the land, and his gentle, tired eyes revealed a thoroughly schooled clerical empathy for the poor. His black beard now flecked with hints of early grey, he wrapped his newish churchman-black cloak around him when the nights grew chilly. On the barge he had watched the land go by, turning to his books when he could, and he had taken his meals with the land-toilers.

The Prava's deep brown waters carried with them the life of the land, and he did not fail to be thankful even when he had accidentally let slip his pipe off the side of the barge. He had been sad, for the pipe had been a gift upon his entry into the order, but he could see the purpose and measure of all things, and his loss was not so great.

At Visselno his assistant had met him with the oxcart. This was a favor from the lord of Scoms, Istan Famm. Together the priest and his assistant rode in the straw-filled rear while two sturdy young village men steered the cart through the rutted tracks and forded the shallow streams that came down from the mountains. The streams would find their way into the muddy Prava, and then past Visselno, over the priest's lost pipe, and far to the south, past his home at Riadom. There the Prava joined with the Leva, and together they flowed south, soon leaving Thane behind and disappearing into the land of the Masters.

The Masters... The priest had for his whole life walked in fear and deference to the blue-skinned race of geniuses who ruled the whole world. They rode through Thane on great stallions and walked the better streets of Riadom draped in gold. On one occasion some years ago he had seen the imperial emissary close enough to tell by his red pupils that he was truly of the superior race. It was the only time in his life that he was sure he had really seen one. Thanian lords might imitate them, but they could not mask their own lower-rung blue or brown eyes. In truth it did not matter that one was a land-toiler or a lord, because all Thanians lived in thrall to the Masters. This was *their* land, in a way, except that ordinary men and women still lived and toiled in these places: Riadom, Visselno, the lands between the Prava and the Leva, and all the poor mudpit villages from which the Thanians sent their crops to enrich the tables of the empire.

As a priest he served the True Belief, which the Masters had given Thane when they forced the land from ignorance. Many ranks of betters stood over him. The line of hierarchy ran from the lowly village priest up through the higher orders to the lord of Riadom himself, who served the great imperial Masters in the distant city of Sarai.

As the oxcart approached the dismal town, the priest's assistant pointed out the fort of Lord Famm. A single tower jutted up from the massive but crude stone walls, which appeared stained and rotten with age. In every direction lay vast fields where the trees had been cleared for tilling. Silent figures worked the fields on their hands and knees, stabbing sticks into the soil to make room for the seedlings, plucking grasses and weeds, and working into their clothes and skin the mud of the land. It would be ineradicable.

The villagers welcomed him with gifts of chickens and hardcrust bread. At dawn the next morning he stood on a stump outside his tiny wooden house in the center of their cluster of shacks that formed the heart of the village while they kneeled before him in obiesance. It was just as the schoolmasters had taught him it would be. The villagers received his wisdom in silence as God's light created the blessed new day. They brought him a sickly new baby wrapped in blankets, whose mother lay resting in a nearby shack. He held the baby up over his head to receive the light of the new day, and he kissed it gently on the cheeks.

"Thank you sower," the baby's own father said with great humility, with his seven other children grasped tightly around him. The baby's lips and fingers were blue and yellow. The priest grieved within already for it. He knew it might not last another day. He did not need to open his books now. He recited the Hyacinth's prayer for ill children in the original holy language of the Masters while the villagers listened silently. Then he repeated it in the rougher Thanian tongue so that they might understand his words.

> God help this child who knows the love of family
>
> God help this child to grow and breathe and live
>
> God help this child to better serve His will
>
> God help this child to be strong and be humble
>
> God bless with his Light all this family

When he handed the little bundle back to the father he whispered his own personel blessing: "May you be humble in God's light."

"Thank you, sower, thank you. My whole family thanks you."

"The village thanks you!" Shouted a woman who stood at the rear of the congregants.

They gathered at the edge of the fields to cremate the little boy at dawn the next day. It was gloriously cloud-free and holy then, and the priest lit the fire with another prayer in the Masters' tongue. These were the words that the Hyacinth had spoken long ago in Sarai as her executioners came for her, and he did not know whether the Thanian language could encompass the great depths of joy and sadness that ringed the verses. This prayer he could not translate for the villagers. It was forbidden.

*   *   *

The priest kept largely to the contemplative routines he had learned as a boy and mastered as a young man in the seminaries and schools of dusty

Riadom. Every sunrise he walked with the land-toilers out to their work amid the crops of Lord Famm and blessed them as the first morninglight shone across the fields.. He spoke with them, tried to learn their names, and when the spirit moved him he took a place beside them, rousting rabbits and tending to the crops. He reminded them of the dignity of their lot, and the humble place of man in God's great work. He supped with them, complimented their children when the children behaved, and saw them through sickness and pain. When the elder of the blacksmiths fell ill with a fever, the priest kept a vigil with the man's young wife and children. When the blacksmith died, the priest took to collecting donations from both the village and, by a stroke of courage, from the hand of Istan Famm, who could hardly hide his surprise at the request for food for the woman. Famm's face was a strange union of human and Master. It had long become the custom among the noble houses to paint themselves in the guise of the Masters, and even in the distant lands of the mountain district Lord Famm kept carefully to this practice. His skin, dyed carefully blue with secret oils, shone greasily in the lamplight of the great room. His hair, likewise colored a dirty white, hung in knots on his shoulders.

"Take her this," Famm had said. "As a token of my respect for the Church." He handed the priest the round loaf of black bread from the center of his table. The lord had then stalked from the room.

The priest's work was not all toil and warmth. It was the nature of the land-toiler, he supposed and had been taught all his life, to be listless and to drink. That they should beat their children and their women was a regrettable fact, but it was not against the law. That they should steal was another matter. Not more than a month after the priest arrived in the town, and only the night after he gave his first church-holiday sermon, to which the land-toilers had come with piety and fear, a land-toiler woman knocked on his door and begged that he intervene with the Lord's men.

The priest's assistant, who slept on a straw mat on the floor beside the door, tried to shush her and make her go away, but the priest awoke and looked out from his bed at the two figures in the firelight.

"I said not to disturb him!" The assistant hissed.

"Please tell the sower," she begged. "They've come for my brother! They say he stole grain from the Lord's own stores!"

The assistant hit her and pushed her toward the door. "Listen to me, woman!" She cried out, and the assistant cursed.

The priest got out of bed. "I am awake, woman. You are Bonnet, yes? The shepherd's wife?"

"Yes, sower! They came to my brother's house! They accuse him of stealing! *Please*, sower! Please come!"

He put on his black robe and followed her to the shack where her brother's family lived. Famm's men had already taken her brother, whose name was Tallet, and now a small group of land-toilers murmured among themselves and comforted Tallet's wife and three children. The wife, fully pregnant, pleaded with the priest to save her husband's life. "They'll kill him, Father! What'll I do?"

The priest had been warned by his elders, who feared that he might not have the strength for his post, not to coddle wrongdoers or their kin. Law was law, and the Church preached fealty. The priest ran his fingers through his thick black beard as he remembered the admonition against undue pity, and knelt beside the woman.

"Did he steal?"

The wife said nothing. Her children clung to her dress. She looked down.

"Teach your children, then, about right and wrong! Their father may not have the chance."

*   *   *

The priest ran through the town, past the wooden shacks and the knotty trees that overhung the road. His assistant followed, trailed in turn by a cottle of curious land-toilers, and out just past the last hut they came upon Famm's men. They had beaten Tallet quiet, and two of them carried him by the arms as his feet dragged lamely behind him. Their leader was a brute by the name of Richard, whose thick arms and callused hands were the terror of the land-toilers. He had grown up among them to be a bully, and recognized as such by the old Sheriff, he had become Sheriff in turn. He stood at least a full head over the priest.

"We've one for the hanging tree," Richard told the priest when he saw him. "Keep those people back!" He turned back threateningly toward the land-toilers, who retreated toward the village. Out along the road, at the bottom of the hill on which Famm's fort stood, there was an ancient oak. Leafless and dead, its strong branches served Lord Famm's will.

"Has the man confessed?" The priest asked. He recognized the prisoner as one who had sat in the front of the congregation the day before, praying as intently as any. Now his bruised face bled, and terror filled his stupefied eyes.

"Not yet," Richard replied. "He is a drunk and a loafer, but we found this!" Another of Famm's men held out a sack of grain to the priest. In the moonlight the priest saw that it was a plain hemp sack that could have come from anywhere.

"Out of the way, churchman," Richard said derisively, spraying the priest with his spittle. "Wait at the hanging tree if you want to be of use."

Richard approached the priest, who now looked up at him.

"Let me speak with him," the priest said. Richard grunted warily to his men, and they threw Tallet down. The priest knelt beside him and took a handful of his greasy hair. The priest whispered angrily. "You're a waste and a wretch if you lie to me, friend! You'll hang, and your family will starve. You're a pious man, if a drunk, and I expect the truth. Now tell me, did you take this sack?"

Tallet blazed with fear. He breathed heavily, then whispered. "Yes, sower. I don't know why."

Richard smiled and removed a whip from his belt. "You've done a better job than I, churchman. I thought he might never confess. *Take him*!"

"Sower!"

The priest filled with horror. Standing over the pleading Tallet. All around him Lord Famm's men laughed. Richard called for a rope. The hanging tree waited. The priest stammered an objection, his hands flew about like butterflies, but Richard would not listen.

"You'll not teach the land-toiler with mercy, Churchman. Mercy or rewards. I've heard about you. You're fresh from the city. You don't know these scoundrels like I do. They learn only by example."

The priest threw himself onto the thief. He looked up at Richard and Famm's men. "He's a sinner, yes. But he has a wife and children to feed, and I'll not see them suffer! It's the brew that led him to this!" To Tallet, who lay motionless beneath him, he said, "Will you swear not to drink? Will you swear before God?"

"*Yes*!"

Richard snorted. "All right, Father. You want to save this man? You want to protect his whore and his rats? Here's your chance."

He held out the whip. "You administer a good solid punishment. Teach him respect for the good Lord Famm."

The priest refused. Richard's men seized Tallet and the priest ran after them. Richard told his men to stop. The priest accepted the deal with a whisper. He took the whip and unraveled it. The oily leather felt strange in his bookish hands. He had never held one before. Uncertain, he looked at Richard, who stood uncomfortably close to him. "Go on, churchman!" Richard snarled. "Teach this pig the Church's position on theft!"

The priest quavered. Richard reached for the whip. The priest jerked it away from him. He looked down at the thief. Then he raised the whip high over his head and brought it down with a *crack* on Tallet's back. The thief cried out, and looked up at the priest in amazement.

"Father!" Tallet cried out. "Father please--"

"You've a duty under God, friend!" The priest said. His voice barely escaped his lips. "To be humble!"

Crack.

"To work!"

Crack.

"To bear your burdens and act like a man of God!"

Crack. Crack. Crack.

With every stroke the priest looked to Richard, and with every stroke Richard demanded another. The priest complied, and admonished the thief with every blow to remember that this was for his own good, for the good of his children, and the good of his soul. Finally his strength failed him. Richard was not satisfied. The priest begged for Tallet's life, but Famm's men easily pushed him aside and laughed at his demands. So Famm's men dragged the priest along with them, and the thief, to the hanging tree at the foot of the fort of Lord Famm, and when they tied the rope around the thief's neck and hoisted him into the air, the priest prayed and prayed for the man's absolution. He prayed for an end to crime and theft, and for the abolition of brew, and he prayed for the good of the family of Tallet and swore that he would provide for them, and faintly and at the end of his prayer, as Famm's men pushed him away and back toward the village, he prayed that he might forget himself and this night, and his own immeasurable fear.

The body of the thief hung for three days, as was the custom of justice in the mountain district. The priest could not forget. He brought food for the family of Tallet, and preached ever harder against the traditional brew, but when he slept he saw the man's face, saw the kicking legs and the laughing Sheriff Richard, and felt once again the oily whip in his own guilty hands.

At dawn on the fourth day the villagers cut the body down and carried it to a prepared pyre at the edge of the field. The first rays of the new rising sun were on the body when the priest put the torch to the oil-soaked bed of dry branches on which the broken body of Tallet the thief now lay.

"Many, many years ago," he intoned with great sadness and shame, with his voice constricted near to a whisper, "a young girl lived with her family in a far distant land. She was not a Thanian, she did not look like us, but she was a girl all the same, and she took ill and died when she was only nine years old. Her family mourned in their own way I guess, as you would, and as we all do, and they went on living, as we will here today. But something happened to her that had never happened before. She did not stay dead, but after three days in the grave she returned. She told them that she had seen a great light that permeated through everything. She had walked in this light in a strange land where she had never been. She had seen many people there who were long dead, and she told her family that the light had come straight from the heart of God almighty. This was a light of love and forgiveness, and she said that she could feel God's presence in the light, and that after she walked and talked to the spirits of the dead the light had told her to come back and tell the world about it. This is what she did. This is how we know that no matter what we suffer in this world and no matter what sadness comes down upon us, that there is something greater that shines through all of us. We cannot see it and cannot feel it except when we open ourselves and let ourselves believe that it is there. Tallet's wife and family must do this now -- indeed we all must do it -- because the burden of pain is too great for simple people like us to bear. You know that Tallet was a good man who treated his wife and his children well. He was a good man in the fields too, but we know that he drank and he made one terrible mistake that cost his life. I know this. I was there when he died. If he could reach out to us now he would tell us that the great light in which he now walks shines through everything. He will see his children again one day. He will. He will always be their father. He would tell them now if he could, that the burden of right-acting is a small one to bear, that the burden of our rightful place -- as faithful people, as toilers on the land, as fathers and mothers -- this is a small burden too. That little girl who first told the world what she had seen beyond death, we call her the Hyacinth now, because her spirit was that of a precious and rare flower. There is joy and freedom in the next world, she tells us. I will tell you that the only way to be sure of that is to obey your betters, pray now for greater faith in the light of God, and keep hope close to your heart."

  The flames devoured the body as the wind picked up.

  "Renounce the brew!" The priest cried out. "Accept your place!"

  Then he recited the Hyacinth's final prayer. None of the mourners understood his words. That hardly mattered now. The priest understood them. He needed to pray today. That the Hyacinth had, herself, been from the race of the Masters not one of the land-toilers questioned.

  It was not their place to do so.

Chapter One: "I WAKE"

She might have jumped from her bed with the suddenness of the thought that roused her. She lay there beneath thick sheafs of sheepskin sewn together with leather strands, her breath rolling in a cloud over her face. She closed her eyes again and for the first time in her life she feared going back to sleep. She pulled her feet and hands close to her body for warmth, the chill of the night still in them. At least it was no longer the winter, when ice caked the walls and she had to pull her frozen robes into the bed to thaw them before she could dress. No, the winter was over. Now the snows came only occasionally. She could begin again to hope for release, for escape, for freedom. These things were denied her family, seemingly for all time.

Petra Harkess rose and wrapped herself in a heavy sheepskin robe. She tied her sheepskin boots tight around her feet, which still felt cold, and she made her narrow wooden-frame straw and sheepskin blanket bed as she had been taught. She sat on the bed and brushed her long black hair.

She was seventeen years old. She had refused marriage. The storm of the thing that woke her still loomed in her mind.

I wake, it had said.

That was what it felt like. Not a dream. Not a memory. She had few memories that were different at all from yesterday and the day before, and from what this day too would bring. Every day of her seventeen years had been the same, and every year of every generation had been the same for her family. In exile from the world, consigned to the remote Monastery on the secret island, living out quiet and cursed lives in the constant memory of the ancient heroes who had led them here, and then left them here.

I wake, it had said with a resonance that scared her. What wakes? There was only one thing that mattered, and in all her years and all the years of her family's exile it had never once spoken. She shook her head and frowned. What a prideful thing I am. Whatever the dream had been, it had certainly not been *that*. Once she had fancied herself a seer. She had imagined prophecies and visions, and in her foolishness she had believed them.

"I am a humble woman," she said aloud. "I am the daughter and the sister. I am the one who shall remain."

She hung her head. She remembered the oath she had taken to her parents. No more foolishness. She had refused marriage. She sat on her bed in the tight cubical stone chamber. The thick wooden shutters were supposed to keep out the light, the sea-winds, and in winter the deathly cold. She reminded herself to tell her father that they needed fixing.

I wake.

This was just more foolishness. She used a short soulfish bone to tie her hair up in a tight bow. She pulled on it until she could feel pain in every strand of her hair. That was just right. Then she stood up again and the smell of woodsmoke from the great room lured her for a morning meal. She closed the thick wooden door behind her and might well have floated from memory alone down the narrow corridor where all the sleeping chambers lay. These were the residences once of brothers and sisters who now lay in the ground at the bottom of the hill on which the Monastery stood. All were gone now but for Petra and her brother.

She greeted her father and mother, the Lord Larniku and the Lady Ysana, with the proper grace of a young Lady of the Harkess clan. They sat together in the warmth of a great fireplace so large that Petra could stand unbent within it if she wished. They bowed their heads slightly to her and and wished her good morning. Her mother's long grey hair flowed down over her robe like something fully alive, and her kind face seemed not to have changed in its capacity for love even as the years of futile waiting gradually reduced her spirit to silence. Her father seemed always to be locked in some grim state. His regard for her had not recovered since her humiliation of the bridegroom, the villager Jindobrei.

"Morning daughter," he muttered.

"Yes my Lord and Lady," she replied with the proper and expected sweetness. "It is a good morning."

"Eat," her father said. "Today we pray on Mericet's bones."

High on the wall that faced the west, the famous stained glass image of the Wheel shimmered with the grey light that penetrated the clouds and the shadows of the cliffs that stood between this island and the rest of the world. Eight round panels around the circumference of the Wheel portrayed the stations of life. One deep red panel in the center, larger than the rest, signified the hub.

Her mother had impressed on her with no small firmness that she rested on the outside. Her father and her brother and her husband might be the hub. Petra, as a lady and a dutiful servant of her family, would not ever be and should not ever pretend to be. This was her sin in their eyes. First with the seer games, and now with the marriage games. This is what they saw in her: a troublemaker, an ingrate, a insolent girl whom they had spoiled and from whom they must now reap their just shame.

She knew this.

I wake.

She shook the words from her mind.

*   *   *

Beneath the Monastery lay two caves. The preferable one emitted warm wet air all through the year. This is what made the island a refuge in the cold sea beyond the world's edge: it had been blessed with hot water at its core, which in addition to heating a crystalline pool in the warm cave below the Monastery and providing life-giving warmth even when the worst ice storms covered the island in a thick freeze, fed warm springs down on the lower slopes toward the inlet that the islanders used as a harbor for their fishing boats. There was only one Monastery. The servants of the Harkess family lived in tiny villages. The hot springs gave them life.

On the slope below the Monastery the ancient monks who had hosted Petra's family long ago had built a rectangular pool and at one end they had fashioned the statue of a ram's head. Hot water flowed from the ram's head in a constant fountain that enabled the villagers to keep their sheep and goat flocks alive during the worst times, and no one on the island failed to recognize its blessings. In the coldest days the steam from the ram's head pool poured into the air and villagers might rest in the huts that they had built around it. Another hot spring down closer to the inlet provided the sustenance for a second village, this one where the fisher families hid themselves when the sea ice kept them from their tasks. Hot water also bubbled out into the inlet itself, so that at all times it attracted fish and eels for the taking. Even during the worst of winter the fishermen might spear their take as they stood on the rocks that jutted out into the steaming water.

There was another cave. This was not the preferable one. In this cave the bones of the famous Harkess heroes rested for all time. Tradition and practice among the Old Believers of Thane held that the bodies of the dead should be interred in the earth in tribute to the Wood. Even though they lived as exiles and had no contact with the spirits of the Wood since their flight some generations ago, the Harkess family had done just that: every child and woman and man who died on this wretched island went into the earth accompanied by the song of the spirits as best the islanders could reproduce it. This is where Petra's brothers and sisters were, and her grandparents and cousins and all the rest, save the firstborn sons of the family. These waited together for their return to Thane. The skeleton of the first and greatest hero, Mericet Harkess, sat in a kingly pose in a small wooden chair, facing the south as if to face his old enemies who now ruled Thane: the Devils and their traitor Thanian allies. Mericet was not quite just a skeleton: the skin of his face had become black and leathern and pulled tight across his skull. Ragged brown robes hung from his frame, which had lost all its substance in the long years of its rest, and now seemed hunched and decrepit. His hands had become black wisps as well, the bones enclosed in skin that had become like the most delicate ash. On the wall beside the body of Mericet Harkess hung his relics: the battle-worn and noble sword with which he had fought at the final battle in the lost war against the invaders, the helmet that he had worn every day of his exile as he prepared to fight again, thick metal-studded leather body armor that now seemed as time-beaten and weak as his body. Another leathern and decayed body sat in a chair beside Mericet. This was his son Taius, who made the crossing of the sea as a boy in his mother's arms, and who stood by his father's side until death took them both in the same year, the father from age and grief, the son from a killing fever. Beside Taius, in another chair bound in shadow, sat the body of his own son Visser. He led the Harkesses in battle when the monks would no longer accept them as true lords, and in the end all the monks died by the hands of Harkess fighters. The family and its servants took over the Monastery, its followers established governance over the villages, and monks fell away into the din of memory.

After Visser, din it became. Petra had never memorized the long list of Harkess lords who did not merit their own chairs in the chamber, for room ran short with the Wheel set into the stone floor and Mericet's vanguard could not accommodate even one more revered personage. No, a long wooden shelf ran the length of the darkest inner wall of the cave, opposite the display of Mericet's relics, and on the shelf, which had first only run part of the length of the wall but had by necessity been extended once and again and again to make room for more, lay the skeletal remains of every one of the men who had reigned over the island since Visser. At least twenty bodies lay in the shelf. All earned their place in the vanguard. All would one day return with their fathers and sons to be interred in a land that none had seen, in honor of the holy Wood, whose spirit emissaries none had ever seen.

Petra kneeled at her mother's side. They bowed down low and rested their foreheads on the cold stone floor, around the edge of the Wheel. Her father kneeled too, on the other side of her mother, and beside him kneeled Petra's brother Vandar. Strangely, two of Vandar's friends had joined the ceremony and crowded in behind Vandar. These were Torjek and Koeno, who had been her brother's companions since childhood, and who were like members of the family in her parents' eyes, and defenders of the islanders. They had lost a fourth friend, Lazar, also like a brother (and the kindest of all in Petra's eyes, except perhaps for Vandar himself), in a fight with a waterman on the edge of the fisher-village before the last winter. Petra had sung with the whole island as they placed him into the earth.

As she sung now. The whole of the remains of the Harkess family joined their voices together in a single unified tone. She hoped that it would be different this time, but she knew beforehand that it would not. They raised their voices together, raised them fervently and with more emotion and more desire.

We are your servants.

Command us.

Petra did not notice the exact moment that Lord Harkess, without warning, stopped singing. She kept to it as she kept to all her obligations now, with a conviction that the meaning was greater than she might immediately perceive, and when she noticed that he had stopped and raised his head the others were already aware.

Lord Harkess rose to his feet. He stood before the hubstone, where no spirit had every made itself visible, and something in him seemed larger and more vital than she had ever seen before. It was something new and indomitable in him. It was his *refusal*.

"Fathers," Lord Harkess addressed his gathered dead forebears. "I am Larniku, your son and defender. I have borne the Harkess shield my whole life, as you did, and I have sworn your vow, Mericet, to return to Thane and reestablish on its land the dominion of the Wood. Harkesses have always hewn to the Wood. Harkesses always shall. I tell you today because you went before in the vow. I tell you this: our family is dying. We have lost seven children in this family. Perhaps their spirits are known to you. They were sweet babies all. We are not the only family on the island to lose children. No, all the loyal families are shrinking, dying. I do not know what the next generation will bring. My vow is to return to Thane. I tell you today that we are going to fulfill that vow. Tomorrow my son departs to cross the sea. I tell you so that you will hear it from me, your own son and heir. It is my decision."

Now she saw the reason that Torjek and Koeno had joined them. Great anxiety filled her. She heard it again: *I wake.*

"Son, step forward," Larniku Harkess said next as he removed the silver medallion from around his own neck. This Wheel-shaped symbol of the Harkess family hung from a strong silver chain, and as Petra scoured her memory of the far recesses of the past it had always hung from her father's neck.

No more.

She could hardly contain her emotions. She hung her head down and pressed her forehead to the stone floor. She heard Vandar taking a new oath before Mericet and Taius and Visser and the others.

"In honor of you I shall take these companions to seek justice in Thane. For you, Mericet, I leave my own blood on the hubstone."

He removed a knife and made a small cut in the palm of his left hand. He wiped the blood across the smooth hubstone. Then Torjek stepped forward. He offered his blood in memory of Taius. Then Koeno offered his to Visser.

It was all wrong.

Now her father spoke again: "Mericet, you fought at the last battle against the invaders. You saw the holy witness float over the field. Our son Vandar shall seek a new fight in honor of all the men who died there and all those who have suffered since. May the Wood send a witness to what he will achieve: the end of the false church, the end of the traitor lords, the end of the Devil empire. Will you take that vow, Vandar?"

"I swear it now, father!"

No, no, no.

Then all the men dropped back to their knees in respect to the dead lords, these same lords whose vow had been to await summons, to preserve strength, to return when called. This was the vow of Mericet Harkess: that no man would return to Thane until the Wood commanded it. For all that her father said about the dying families on the island, which she knew was true and she knew that the poor prospects for the future fell partly to her refusal to marry, the one immutable fact was this: the Wood had issued no summons, no command. Her voice screamed inside her: "Why do you act so precipitously? Why do you ignore your vow?" She would have said something to this effect, but she knew that they would not listen.

She pressed her head down on the stone.

Wishing for silence inside.

Chapter Two: The Dark Crevasse

Vandar Harkess, the last son and heir to the House of Harkess, walked out from the Monastery along the crumbling rock trail that led to the northern hills of the island. He wore a light cloak of frayed sheepskin, and carried with him a sack of food and, hanging from his belt, a simple short sword that he had received from his father upon his engagement to the girl Anjelica, from the village of the herders and farmers. It was not affixed with jewels, as the ancient lords might have preferred their weapons, because those things did not exist on the island. It was plain and decorated only with the eight-pointed Wheel of the Thanian religion as it was practiced on the island: the Old Belief. The eight stations of the Wheel represented the stations on the journeys of life, and the central hub represented faith itself. He wore the Wheel also on a silver medallion, a gift from his father.

Vandar had broken faith. He would be gone within a day.

The wind whipped at him from the sea, which crashed on the rocks at the bottom of the cliff on which the Monastery stood, and his hair blew about with each gust. His face was thin and hawklike, his eyes round and blue. His cheekbones made jagged angles just below his eyes, and his whole face seemed to narrow down to his thin mouth and his sharp, jutting chin. His eyes were his mother's, and his face and wiry frame his father's. He was not a large man, but he was young and strong, and he took each step of the path, when it angled sharply up along the grassy bluff, at a swift and agile pace.

The whole island seemed to confine him. He looked back at the Monastery, with its white stone roofs and grand stained glass window (again in the form of the Wheel), and the outbuildings that lined the interior of the low stone perimeter wall. This crumbling structure embodied all that Vandar hated about the island, about his family and father, and the curse that robbed the Harkess name of vitality and glory. They had survived the conquest of the Devils, perhaps, but they had lost their courage. Now they were slowly dying.

The Island of the Monastery lay just beyond the northern edge of the world. It lay in a cold sea in the shadow of the world's great cliffs, which rose up to staggering heights and blocked out the sun and sky during the worst months of winter. At the top of the cliffs, which the islanders had long ceased to imagine or contemplate, lay the world itself: warm and idealized in fireside stories, longed-for by the romantic and glory-seeking, and forever beyond their reach. Their island lay at the foot of those cliffs, beneath the grey clouds that collected mid-way up the rocky face. It was forever cold and windy and wet, forever cut off from the world itself, and forever alone in the long night of Thane's enslavement.

The people of the island had no idea what had happened in Thane since their own ancestors fled the place centuries before. They knew the stories of the Devil armies, the witness at Coormo, the betrayal of their lands by the traitors in Riadom and Visselno, and the long flight of the Harkesses across Thane. They knew the name Mericet Harkess, who inherited the mantle of the house of Harkess after his father's death in battle, and who led the family and its servants through the forests and hills of the frontier, into the Mountains at the End of the World, and down through a secret tunnel that led into the dark earth. At the end of it they found the sea, a hidden crevasse with boats for the taking, and the island itself.

For three hundred years they had lingered here, and not once had an islander set foot on the land back across the strait. *The world is cursed*, Mericet Harkess had said when claiming the island for his family, *and we shall no more return to it than we will sell out ourselves to the monsters who now rule it.* He decreed that death should be the punishment for any who dared return to the world before the Wood's command, and set about to build himself a contemplative tower on the far northern tip of the island. This place, which he called Heart's Ease, watched out on the northern seas, which extended out into darkness and infinity, beyond sight or understanding. There were no more islands, and no more men or women to be seen out there. There was only peace and silence, and the endless moment in which to savor nothingness.

Vandar looked back at the Monastery. Beyond it was another round and grassy hill. This was really just the southern end of a long a treeless ridge that lined the west side of the island, in the center of which stood the old Monastery. Shepherds grazed their flocks on the southern hill, tiny figures wrapped in sheepskin cloaks to keep out the damp chill. It was a cloudy and windy day on the island of the Monastery, just like every other day.

The eastern slope of the ridge, below the Monastery, ended in a tangle of pastures and farming fields, then gave way to the forest that covered the rest of the island. The trees stretched out in a great mass of green towers, and the sea took up beyond.

Between the ridge and the forest lay the villages of the Harkess clan. Directly below the Monastery lay the village of the herders and farmers around the pool of the ram's head. It was they who grazed their sheep along the ridge, and they who coaxed potatoes from the cold ground. At the southern end of the island, at the foot of the slope of the southern hill, lay a small harbor and the village of the fishermen. Their longboats sailed at dawn every day, and the fish they pulled from the sea graced every table on the island. There were scut and murmurer in these waters, and the soulfish (whose belly glowed as it died), and the floater, which yielded a week's worth of food for the whole island if it could be hauled back to the harbor. They were huge but rare, and the capture of a floater usually meant a holiday for the fishing village.

This was the island of the exiles. The Harkess lord in his Monastery, the farmers and shepherds, the fishermen. All descended from the Harkesses who fled Thane, all safe from the slavery imposed by the Devils, all alone on their dank and remote island, in the shadow of the cliffs of the world itself. How high did those cliffs go, Vandar wondered as he gazed upward, over the Monastery, at the sheer rock face and the clouds that gathered up against it. They could rise no further, yet far beyond them lay all that mattered to him as a future lord and a man. There lay the Devils and the land of Thane. There lay the monsters who stole the world. There lay his future.

Vandar had taken another vow before Mericet. He knew the old man's face now, and he understood that Mericet might have forbidden him to leave the island. He was glad that his father Larniku was lord now. He could see that Vandar had a greater contribution to make than to sit forever in exile.

He had broken faith. He would never return.

*   *   *

The longboats left the village of the fishermen just past dawn. Vandar watched them go. They rowed out from the safety of the harbor and onto the roiling sea. Huge swells passed as a matter of course beneath the boats, whose masters were well accustomed to steering over them. When they neared the great wall of the world the swells became trickier and more violent. The fishermen dropped long hooks down into the depths while their rowers kept the boats from hitting the rock wall. This was a dangerous life. Many times boats had collided with the rocks, or overturned when crazy waves met beneath them, and not many and islander could swim.

Not so rare, and just as deadly, were the things that dropped from the sky. High above them at the tops of the cliffs walked animals and perhaps people. How long did it take for rocks dislodged by footfalls along the edge of the world up there take to fall out of sight, through the cloud layer, and down into the sea itself? How many Thanian boats had been punctured by the projectiles that fell from the sky? And it was not always rocks. It could be a deer (which had happened once), or a man (which had not happened yet). Any large object could prove fatal to the inhabitants of a fishing boat from the island.

Some fishermen did not watch the sky. They trolled the shallow waters on the landward side of the island itself, and they did their hunting with spears. They wrestled with the pumafish and snarkers that sometimes preyed in those waters, and they had lost more than one man to the poisoned tentacles of the loathsome watermen, which walked like men on the bottom of the sea, very like the damned of the world itself. Certain families had taken the shallows as their place, and these were the risks they ran, just as the others who knew the rock faces of the world ran their own risks. It was the way of the Thanians to fish where they would (said these Harkess clansmen), and they had no use for fear.

"May our swords be good and our words be good," went the anthem of the Harkess family. "May the Wheel turn."

*　　　*　　　*

The rowers pulled on their oars and the skiff gained speed. Within the confines of the harbor of the south village, it moved smoothly along the flat surface of the cold water. It moved past the south hill, away from the distant Monastery and its villages, and out toward the open sea.

They had made their goodbyes simple and quiet. Love to parents, love to brothers (for Vandar, none), love to sisters (just the forever silent Petra), and a vow of return. As Vandar left his parents and sister to whatever their future might be and walked down the long hill toward the fisher-village, his father had followed him for a few steps and taken him by the arm. "One final word from your father, son," Lord Harkess had said with the air of a man who realized that he would not see his son again. "Do not lose your honor!"

"I won't, father. Thank you."

The adventurers met at the edge of the fisher-village. where, as a final gift, the fisherman father of their friend Lazar had agreed to transport them to the hidden crevasse where they would begin their journey. Lazar's father steered the boat now, as Torjek and Koeno rowed. Vandar sat at the prow, studying the cliffs with a new and more urgent sense than every before.

The clouds hung in the sky, and the rock face of the world was like the walls of a pit. All around the small boat, which went out of the harbor and onto the blue sea, the waves grew larger and more crafty. Mericet Harkess had stood at the island's northern point and wondered if there lay another sanctuary, another land to which they ought to flee. He had decided against it. Many years later, Vandar had stood very near the same spot and wondered what sort of a boat it might take to reach the far side of the northern sea (the existence of which he had postulated to a reasonably firm degree). How many days worth of food and water? How many oarsmen? The most important question was this: would one ever reach a place that was beyond the sight of the cliffs of the world? Would one pass beyond that point?

Vandar thought about those questions as the boat went out into the straits. The salty air whipped across his face and the faces of his companions. He had sworn that they would escape the island, that they would all be free men together, that he would return to Thane and fight the Devils and die like a man. His two friends Torjek and Koeno came with him. All three of them were made tough by the endless winters on the island, when ice made everything slick and deadly, when the ice accumulated along the interior walls of every home, when the frozen corpses of the dead lay endlessly in their pallets awaiting the damp springtime, when the cold and lonely souls gathered and prayed over the Wheel, when steam poured off the ram's head pool, when one could walk on the frozen sea out far from the island without fear of slipping into the depths and being consumed by the watermen, and when the icy fingers of the wind pushed lovers together from confinement and lust. "We will walk together as men," they had said on their last night on the island, when they drank wine in the wood and saw no future but their own. "We three friends. May our swords be good and our word be good. May the Wheel turn!"

Now Vandar looked back toward the island of the Monastery with a feeling that was oddly sad. He had passed his whole life there, but that life was over. He had left his father and mother and sister in the ancient and still hilltop Monastery, and the said farewells would never be enough. To his father he had little left to express. In truth, had his father not blessed his journey he might have fled anyway. To his mother all that was possible had long since passed between them. To his sister, however, whose visage was like death and whose love was locked away inside her, he had a sudden and clear sense of failed responsibility. He could no longer look out for her, no longer protect her from the barbs of the other islanders, no longer be her only friend.

There was guilt in his heart, but only a little. The Wheel had turned. He had no place on the island any longer.

The cries of black birds circling high overhead caught Vandar's attention, and he looked up at the endless rock wall, the world-cliff's face, and the circling birds called to one another and flew up the rock face on winds. They became specks against the grey wall, and their cries were lost in the roar of the waves against the distant cliffs, the lapping of the water against the skiffs and the oars. Concern intruded on Vandar: how would they sleep on the boat tonight?

He looked at his two friends, and their faces were frozen in grins of adventure and fear. The wind whipped across them, the waves buffeted them, and their swords were still sheathed, like Vandar's own short sword. Torjek's long blond hair lay in heap around his shoulders, and his black beard seemed to belong to a man ten years older. He looked out across the sea at the cliffs, and back to the island.

"Come with us!" He said to Lazar's father in a sudden rush, but the man only smiled and shook his head. "Thank you my lord Vandar, but I must stay with my family. I have already lost one son. I cannot lose another minute with them. I will steer you there. That will be enough for me."

Vandar nodded in acceptance. His friends rowed on.

"Can you see the Monastery?" Vandar asked.

"It is a safe distance," Koeno said. "We are safe from it now, from the endless sleep of the poor cold island. Let them sleep forever in their peace, but let it be theirs alone!"

"We shall come back to them with news of Thane," Torjek said.

Vandar did not think so.

"Give me the wandering life," He intoned grandly. "Give me a sword and a bottle! Give me a dark night and the howl of wolves, give me a swamp and dogs in pursuit. Give me one day on the field, with my brothers at my side, give me one day of glory. I would trade it all for those things with you, my brothers!"

His voice trailed off and the three of them looked at the cliffs of the great wall of the world. Vandar realized that he did not have to make such claims anymore. He did not have to boast or issue oaths, did not have to swear that his quiet princely life would not do. He did not have to posture anymore, because he had kept his word. He had sworn to leave the island, and he had done it. No man could call him a coward now.

Torjek and Koeno looked at him.

"My your sword be good and your word be good..." said Torjek. He smiled proudly as he said it.

"It *is*, friend! It is!" Koeno laughed. He hooted long and loud, and clapped his hands. The boat rocked underneath them as a strong wave moved toward the cliff. Torjek lurched toward the edge in a moment of lost balance, and Koeno and Vandar both reached for him.

"May the Wheel turn..." Torjek said, finishing the Harkess credo. He slapped at his friends' hands, and then they all three put their hands together.

"We three friends," Vandar said, "we three friends shall see every corner of the world! We shall tramp in the rivers of Thane and leave our mark all across the land. They shall always say: here went those three bastards that stole our daughters and our fortunes, that killed our Devil-lords and set us all to running back home."

Torjek and Koeno laughed. His speech was an old joke between them now, and had been repeated on black nights and in drunken rages, on the last northern hill of the island and in whispers between the friends in a crowded banquet at the Monastery itself. And his friends always laughed. Torjek with his blond hair and black beard, with his stately swordsmanship and his charms for the ladies, whose eyes were like water and whose words could be those of a poet. Koeno laughed too--Koeno the joker, the asp, the night-spirit. Koeno whose talent was mockery and verbal tactics, whose words were like knives, who had been at Vandar's sides since the dawn of consciousness.

Vandar looked back toward the island. *I shall not see you again*, he thought of his father, the Lord Harkess. *Goodbye mother. Goodbye sister.*

Vandar's stomach roiled with the waves as the tiny skiff rolled between them and atop another. He had never been in a fishing boat, never once before this moment. That particular pleasure was banned for the Lord and his heir by the decree of the great Mericet Harkess on the day he landed on the island. It was the sentence of the lord and his sons, that they should remain here until summoned by the Wood. Mericet had abandoned the world and forced his sons to do the same. Never once had the Wood made itself heard. The Harkess lords had all followed his wishes, and had become progressively more docile and weak, and not until this day had one disobeyed the command. Larniku sent them forth because he knew the family was dying. Not until this day had Vandar had his choice in anything in life.

He had chosen freedom. He had chosen the world up above the cliffs. He had chosen the sword.

The Wheel had turned.

They rowed through the silvery moonlit night. When the sun rose, casting its long grey shadows from its place hidden behind the cliffs, they rowed still. No more speeches were heard on the boat. No more boasts.

* * *

The tiny skiff crawled in parallel to the cliffs, and the sun shone from high in the sky at mid-day before they rounded a long outcropping. The three friends took turns at the large steering oar at the flat stern. It was Vandar's turn when they passed around the north-facing tip of this tower of rock. It was like a turret to defend the world against the assault of the cold sea. Vandar studied the grey cliffs, which led upward into the mists, and he wondered what beasts stood at the edge of the world at that very moment, gazing down into nothingness and wondering what would happen if they slipped from their footings. Were they men? Were they Thanians?

Lazar's father steered them all the way. "We're coming to it!" He said. "You'll be there soon!"

As the skiff came around the great outcropping, another long wall of cliffs was revealed to them. Only it seemed to Vandar that there was something different about this view. It was unlike the view that had been available to them on the island. Vandar narrowed his attention on a distant section of cliff wall that now came into view. It was like a great crack in the world, which was narrow where the sea washed up against it but which widened as it reached up toward the clouds. It was a scar, a wound in the earth's side, and Vandar was sure in an instant that it was the spot from which the Harkess clan had sailed out to the island. It had to be.

"Look friends!" Vandar shouted. "The gateway to our homeland!" Torjek and Koeno stopped rowing for a moment and rubbed their sore arms as they looked out across the sea. Their faces were red and they drank thirstily from their watersacks.

It was told in the tale of Mericet Harkess that he led his people down from their pursuers through a great crevasse in the earth, and that at the end of a steep and dark path, they found boats and a dock. They had lost everything, and had had only their honor to warm them in the depths of the crevasse. When they came to the island, they were welcomed by the monks who lived there. It was the monks who built the Monastery, and who sustained it in part through contributions from the Harkess fortune. It was also the monks who were killed by the Harkess fighters after ten years of co-existence, when the lord Visser Harkess established the family's final rule over the island.

The skiff rose atop the swells, and Torjek and Koeno rowed harder in waters that grew more violent as they approached their goal. Lazar's father held onto the steering oar. If the boat were swamped, they would all drown. Not one of them could swim.

The skiff heaved upward with the waves. Vandar's stomach dropped inside him. He held onto the oar. "Closer!" Lazar's father called out to Torjek and Koeno, who rowed harder than ever. They did so without question, without hesitation.

They approached the entrance to the crevasse. High above them, the two sides of it separated and rose in parallel, high up into the grey clouds that overhung the sea. White water poured out of the dark opening in the cliff, then from the sea-side a wave sped through the foam and plunged into the dark crevasse. From within came a great deep *roar*, and all four of the men in the skiff listened quietly.

Vandar exulted. They were so close. So near to the goal. His friends looked to him. White swirls surrounded the skiff now, and swells moved beneath it with such force that Vandar's stomach became sour and confused.

"It is rough today!" Lazar's father shouted. "We should wait!"

"No!" Vandar shouted. "Closer!"

Torjek and Koeno rowed with all their strength. Foam flew up from the water and flecked their faces with white spots. As the tiny skiff approached the dark opening in the rock, another wave plunged into the darkness. This emitted the same rushing roar that they had heard before, but now they were much closer to the source. It was overpoweringly loud, and Vandar tightened with anxiety. The waves were so high, and the violence of the crevasse so clear, that he began to doubt that they could enter it successfully. It seemed like a fatal mission, and he had no wish to die foolishly.

From the mouth of the crevasse poured white foaming backwater. It came in force, and sent a wave of its own back at the sea which met an incoming wave with a loud *CLAP* and spray flew high overhead. Then the wave came at the skiff. Vandar watched the wave descend on them with no reaction at all. The wave moved like lightning, and the bow of the skiff tipped upward as the wave passed under it. The four men grabbed handholds as the skiff rode over the wave and righted itself. Lazar's father kept one hand on the steering oar.

He turned around to watch as the counter-wave raced out to the sea. It met another incoming wave and water splashed up as the two waves CLAPPED together, then each one continued in its direction. The incoming wave passed underneath the skiff and carried it closer to the mouth of the crevasse.

The roar of the waves was overwhelming. The proximity to the cliff walls terrifying. Torjek shouted to Vandar, but Vandar could not make out the words. He understood only the fear in Torjek's eyes. Lazar's father held onto the steering oar, but he could not use it to any effect. It dangled behind the skiff uselessly. He looked up at the cliff walls, and wondered for a brief moment of clarity whether one could climb the cliffs themselves. He looked back at Lazar's father. He could read the man's face.

"We must turn around!" Lazar's father shouted.

Torjet and Koeno rowed together in the swirling waters. Another wave poured out from the crevasse and nearly overturned the skiff. Vandar took no fear this time, but he could not control the skiff. It turned in circles as the waters sucked it toward the crevasse. The crevasse loomed just before them, and they turned in uncontrollable circles. Torjek and Koeno yelled to one another and to Vandar, but he could not make out their words. He recognized the fear, but that was no surprise. He was sure that somewhere down beneath his confusion he was afraid too. There was just nothing he could do to stop what happened next.

Another wave gathered beneath the skiff, and carried it toward the mouth of the crevasse while two of its passengers rowed at cross-purposes and a third sat still in dumb amazement. Lazar's father shouted out to them, but Vandar could not hear him. The sides of the crevasse rose up from the roiling waters like great columns, and the salty wind came out of its mouth like the exhalation of a monster. There was a line between daylight and shadow, a line that the skiff crossed as it rode atop the wave and entered the crevasse itself.

The skiff hurdled forward into the darkness.

Lazar's father dropped his steering oar and gripped the wall of the skiff with both hands. The water was like a god now, and laughing. He shouted to the three friends. "Hold on tight! We're going in!"

Then he and Vandar locked eyes, just for a moment.

The prow of the skiff had, by chance, faced forward in the few seconds that the wave carried it into the crevasse. And the skiff slid down the front of the wave it had cut into the water neatly, and this alone had kept it from overturning at the high speed and crazy angle at which it now traveled. Lazar's father waved Vandar backward, away from the prow. Vandar now stood up nearly straight and leapt backward between Torjek and Koeno. Lazar's father took him by the hand and pulled him to the back of the skiff. Then the prow suddenly plunged beneath the surface of the water. They were swamped. Torjek and Koeno both shouted in panic. Then the force of the wave pushed the back of the boat up over the front.

Vandar rose up over his friends and for a weird instant looked down on them as he passed overhead. Then the skiff came down and water filled his mouth. He was cast free of the boat and sucked into the force of the wave. He went end over end as water sprayed at him from every direction.

It was as if he were flying in a dream.

Chapter Three: In Darkness

Vandar tumbled through the dark waters. His eyes may have been open or closed, and he may have cried out with fear. He may have let go of the skiff, or he may not have. There was no thought in him. There was only the darkness and the water, the vertigo, and the roar of the wave that filled the crevasse and his ears. Heard from within the wave, this was the sound of death for foolish men.

Somewhere near him was a small skiff. He had fallen from it, or he may have jumped from it. He did not know. There was also a hand that hit him in the face as he traveled through the water. It was the hand of one of his two friends, or perhaps his dead friend's father. He could not see which. They both must have been close by him, like the skiff. Caught up in the wave, moving together.

Into the choking darkness.

Vandar scraped along the long rough surface of a stone. The force of the wave compressed his body onto it, and dragged him along it, tearing at his hands and face and legs. Ripping his heavy sheepskin cloak. Then he slammed into another rock, which jutted out at a sharp angle from his scraping-board. The impact was tremendous. His lungs emptied. Water forced itself down his throat. His eyes opened as he choked. The rocks were green and slippery with moss. He was drowning on them.

The force of the water now ceased. What had carried the skiff into the crevasse and tossed it about like a flower had expended all its strength. The power that had compressed Vandar against the green rocks now lifted, and for an instant there was no threat at all in the water. It was cold and salty, but it was not the hand of the drowner, the killer sea. It was merely water. Then it began to drain away, and suddenly Vandar's head was not immersed in water anymore. He breathed in air, to his everlasting surprise, and vomited. Then he found a handhold on the rock. The draining wave washed past him and over him. He held on.

Vandar choked on salt water. He coughed and vomited again, and called out to his friends. "Torjek! Koeno!"

He held onto the slippery rocks, his fingernails dug into waterworn indentations with all the solidity that he could muster. The skin on his face and hands, although he could not see it, was scraped and bloody, and he could not get a foothold. The salt water swirled around his waist, draining away into the sea beyond the crevasse. He struggled for a foothold.

"Torjek!"

He looked back out across the water. What might have been the bottom of the overturned skiff floated in the outgoing water. Vandar considered lunging for it. He tried again to pull himself up out of the water onto the rocks. Another wave was coming. He knew that. It was the only certainty. And if he could not pull himself up onto the higher rocks he would be swept away.

"Koeno!"

Vandar listened for his friends. He heard nothing. He called out again, and when there was no reply his thoughts became more distracted, more concerned. What if they were lost? What if...

Then he saw a body floating in the water just below where he stood. It wore the same red cape that Lazar's father had worn. It circled in the momentarily calm waters, awaiting the rush of the next wave.

"Torjek! Koeno!"

He called out their names desperately, and twisted himself around to look for them in the water. He saw only the overturned skiff and the body of Lazar's father, nothing more. Then he saw what he had feared. At the open mouth of the crevasse, where sunlight shone and the ocean moved like an animal or an angry god, where Vandar and his friends had passed moments before, Vandar saw the swelling of another wave. It seemed to lurk in place for a moment, but then white foam appeared all around it and the deep roar of rushing water rose up around him. The wave hurtled into the crevasse, toward Vandar and the overturned skiff.

Vandar threw himself up on the slippery rocks. He scratched at the moss and cut his fingers on the barnacles, and struggled to find a toehold. Anything to get him up and out of the water. Anything to save himself. There was nothing. Finally he dug his fingers into the holds that he had found, and used his arms alone to slowly pull his body up from the water. His feet dangled uselessly, finally up out of the water, and as he peered over the rocks he could see a wide ledge that disappeared into the darkness of the crevasse. He pulled once again with his hands, and dragged himself up the slippery surface, urged on in desperation by the approaching roar, to escape from the wave that now descended on him.

First it felt like a heavy rain fell on his legs and back, but only for a hair of an instant. Then a tremendous force fell on Vandar from behind, and he lost his handhold on the slippery rocks. The wave crashed onto the rocks and the ledge with the weight of the dark sea itself. In an instant, Vandar was subsumed in water again. The force of the wave threw him up onto the wide ledge, which was just as instantly flooded itself, and he landed hard on another waterworn boulder. He coughed up blood (the taste, he knew it instantly), and inhaled seawater again. He lifted himself up, found that he was breathing air again, and vomited up the seawater. It was tinged with blood. He choked and coughed, and the water began to drain away from him. He thanked God for his life. He was on solid ground. In the darkness of the crevasse, he was on solid ground.

The Wheel had turned.

* * *

Vandar got to his feet. The ledge rocks were slippery and his balance was unsteady on them. He called out for Torjek and Koeno, and looked out at the raging waters.

Even as the force of the last wave dissipated back into the sea, another one gathered beyond the mouth of the crevasse. The capsized skiff spun in circles in the violent waters, and the stench of salt and decay was overpowering. He could not find Lazar's father's body now. There was only a half-light in the crevasse, which was almost more like a tunnel. Although from the sea it had seemed that this place was open to the sky, that the walls of the crevasse rose separately and created a gap in the cliff-wall that widened as it rose upward toward the world, from inside the crevasse seemed dark and sealed. It was like the grave, like the world beneath the world. Vandar scurried along the ledge, looking toward the seaward opening of the crevasse constantly. The next wave would come from there, he knew, at any moment. To his left were the swirling waters. To his right the cold rock wall gave way to an opening into the darkness. He felt along the wall and peered into the dark portal. A steady breeze emanated from it. Vandar backed away from the opening, peering through the shadow-light of the crevasse. This was the way out. It must be, he thought. Confused. He called out his friends' names. Stared into the swirling water of the channel. Kept his stance on the slippery and worn rocks. The overturned skiff turned in its lonely circles. Another wave gathered at the mouth of the crevasse. Vandar cried out to his friends.

"Torjek! Koeno!"

He could not breathe.

"They followed me. They died because of me. All of them."

Then the roar of the approaching wave grew louder and he gazed out at it. The white foam rising up. Racing into the crevasse at him. His footing seemed so poor on the slippery rocks. In the water just before him, which now seemed to feed back into the oncoming wave, he thought he saw the shape of a man. Floating beneath the surface. He could not see who it was or if it was merely an illusion. He scrambled backward on the rocks and lunged for the tunnel. The force of the wave sent a flood of water in after him. He clawed at the dank walls but the backflow was not so powerful. The water drained back away from him and he followed it. Shouting for Torjek and Koeno. Looking down into the water.

Shouting again.

Not believing that they were gone.

*   *   *

The steps went on and on. He crawled sometimes. At other times he pulled himself up to his feet and walked despite the blazing pain that hobbled him. The darkness did not yield, and the difference between day and night became a thing of memory only. There was sleep, which was fitful and full of uncertainty. In the dreams he saw long lines of men walking together across the frozen north sea. They wore red robes and carried the heads of blue-faced corpses on pillows before them. The heads had long white hair, and the robed men bore them like treasure.

Or offerings.

He was in the dream. He floated above the bearers, watching them and invisible to them. He flew up high above them and saw that they were walking toward the distant island of the Monastery. He saw that the lines of men were actually great concentric circles of red robed men, at least five or six of them, one within the other. Centered on the island.

They bore the heads before them, and they sang a song that Vandar had known in childhood:

> Here comes the weeping widow
>
> Look! There goes the mouse
>
> With her broom the weeping widow
>
> Chases it from the house!

Vandar floated high about the concentric red circles. At the center of them all was the island. When he first saw it, the feeling was of fear. But he floated like a bird, and as he rose up it disappeared below the clouds. The red circles could still be seen, and the song could still be heard, but he had no fear.

He rose so fast! He saw the lip of the world approaching, beckoning as he drew nearer and nearer, and he reached out to take hold of it. But then he stopped rising. Something in his stomach seemed to turn upside down, and he flailed as he began to drop back from the lip of the world. He fell away from it with a scream, down toward the clouds and through them, and then he saw the red concentric circles. He was falling right into the center of them, like they were a great target and he was one of his father's darts.

He screamed as the long fall came to an end--

*   *   *

Vandar awoke in the darkness. He clutched at the cramping pains that tore through his legs. Seemed ready to turn them inside out. He thought for a moment that he was dead, that he had died falling from the world's edge, but then his memory came back to him. He was in the endless stairway, he remembered, where thought and mystery lived like demons. He was in the bowels of the world, and he had left his friends far behind him. He had fancied himself a hero and a swordsman, and he was going to die in this tomb. He had thought trying to take the skiff, but even if it had not been smashed by the waves, he would never be able to escape from the crevasse. This he knew for certain. He had been inside it once before. It was a place of death.

Like Lazar's father, and Torjek and Koeno.

What had happened?

"I will die in the earth," he said to himself. He was sure of it. He had given up hope of finding an end to the tunnel, and he had not eaten since the island. His provisions had been enough for ten days (if eaten very sparingly) but they went down in the crevasse, and Vandar had only the dripping water that he could find at occasional intervals along the stair. He found it by feeling along the walls, and wiping the water up with his fingers, then sucking it from them. He tasted metals in the water, but he did not care. He heard dripping and stopped to sate himself, and knew that he would only become weaker and more desperate.

There was no food in the tunnel. No food or light, no sound save the occasional drip of water. Yes, there was the sound that Vandar made: the shuffling of his sheepskin boots, the heavy breathing, the pounding of his heart. Of these things he was less aware. He climbed the steps without counting or a sense of time, and without fear. There was nothing to fear in the endless stair.

Vandar sat down on a step and rested. He had never been so tired. So much in pain. In his legs and feet. He had climbed for an unknown amount of time, and he thought that he should sleep. He wondered how long he could go on without food. The image appeared in his mind of a thick slab of fish meat, cooked over the open fire in the kitchen at the Monastery. He imagined the bubbling juices in which the fish was served, and the potatoes which had been cooked with it. He could almost see the steam rising from the plate, and he further fantasized that he could see his own hand reaching out toward the plate. Reaching for a piece of the fish. His mouth watering at the notion.

Something stirred Vandar from his reverie. He had taken to falling asleep by fantasizing about food, and nothing had disturbed him before. This time was different. He opened his eyes and looked up to the upward stairs. Then he looked down to the downward stairs. He began to laugh at himself: "Foolish you! There is nothing in the tunnel! Nothing at all! That's why I am going to die here!"

Hardly had that thought passed when there came from below, from the way he himself had come, the distinct tap--tap--tap of feet upon the stone steps. Feet in the darkness, where there could be no one. Vandar looked down into the blackness. His eyes might as well have been closed for all he saw, but the instinct to look was too strong. He looked, and what he heard was this:

Tap - tap - tap

They were not running feet, nor feet in any hurry at all. They were merely climbing the steps.

Vandar stood up shouted. "Torjek! Koeno! Is that you?"

He waited.

"Friends! I thought you were dead! I could not find you!"

No reply. Now his hand drifted down to the pommel of his short sword, which had rested in its sheath, hanging from his belt, all this time. He had let his friends die while his sword hung uselessly at his side. Now, for the first time, he put his hand to it. He listened again.

Tap

Vandar stood in the darkness like a blind man in his matted sheepskin cloak and boots. He slowly pulled the sword from its sheath. His father had given it to him when he passed into manhood. Now he would use it. He stood in the darkness, his sword drawn, and awaited whatever it was that followed him. He put his other hand beneath his coat and held the necklace.

Tap - tap

"Torjek?"

Vandar listened and imagined: two feet, walking in the darkness, following me... He lifted the sword up over his head. He could see nothing at all. He might not see the thing before it was on him. Perhaps it was a waterman. If that were the case, he might feel the sting of its poisonous tentacles long before it ever came within reach of his sword. Then his flesh would swell up and his body would stiffen, and he would still be awake as it began to eat him.

Tap

But what would a waterman gain from following him up into the earth? Why would it come this far? Now his mind conjured up every stripe of fearsome thing. Perhaps the channel in the crevasse was a nest of watermen. Perhaps the skiff had traveled right over their heads, and perhaps Vandar himself had only been a moment from death when he was hanging onto the rocks. Perhaps they have followed in their stunted pace, with their gibbering jaws and their mindless red eyes. Perhaps Torjek had fallen directly into their hands. And Koeno too.

Tap - tap - tap

The waterman was an obscenity that walked on the floor of the great sea that surrounded the world, and occasionally wandered up onto the island of the Monastery itself. Its body was that of a man, affixed with swirling poisonous tentacles, but its gibbering mouth knew no language or expression. It existed only to eat and to wander, and those on the island who knew such things regarded the watermen with hatred. They were the souls of the damned, it was said, who came down from Thane to walk forever.

Tap

In the blackness of the endless stair, Vandar Harkess waited with his sword ready to strike. He waited and listened to the footfalls on the stairs below, and he listened for breathing or whispers. He listened and waited, then took a slow step backward, upward, away from his pursuer. Then he turned and slipped up the stairway, his sword still drawn, one hand trailing along the wall for balance. He had seen nothing, but he had heard the footfalls. That was enough. He went on into the darkness without a thought of stopping again, sure now that he would push on until he reached the end or fell dead trying.

* * *

It might have been five days later. This was Vandar's best guess.

His legs moved, his hand felt along the cold wall. He took each step without thinking now, and his feet moved effortlessly beneath him--despite the pain in his legs, the biting hunger, and the thirst that made him lick at the damp walls like a rat.

All the while, his mind conjured images of home.

He saw the Monastery's white walls and majestic position on the ridge, the grassy hills where the shepherds watched over their flocks, the tiny villages where the farmers and fishermen lived, the pool of the ram's head. He listened to the drums and the pipes, with their fluting mysteries, the singers whose voices came from heaven, the deathless credo of the Harkess clan: *May your sword be good and your word be good...*

Their faces were bathed in golden light:

His mother, Ysana, who watched over the island from a favorite place on the parapet of the Monastery, whose eyes were green and whose touch could heal the heart of a child. He saw her now, and her very presence was beckoning.

Come home, she said. *Come back to me.*

His father the Lord Harkess, Larniku, whose grimace was stony and silent, who sat in the cave of the dead lords with his face pressed to the smooth hubstone. Vandar owed his father an explanation for all that had befallen him. All that gone so wrong. Those on the island would know when Lazar's father did not return.

Then he saw his sister, Petra, whose soul was alive but far away, and who saw all worlds together. Their father had silenced her, but to Vandar's mind perhaps they should have consulted her before embarking on this adventure. In his vision she sat alone by the fireplace in the great hall of the Monastery, her black dress fastened tightly around her arms and her neck, and she looked up at the great stained glass panel that oversaw that huge room. She looked up as if counting the stations of the Wheel that was represented in the panel, and to the walking sleeper who saw this, she seemed so beautiful and glasslike. Nine sons and daughters there had been, and only Petra and Vandar survived. Now there would be only Petra, and one day Vandar would be forgotten. Only Petra would live on in the great old Monastery.

He walked on, savoring her gentleness, her peaceable observance of the old Wheel, her delicate and humble way, and as he did this she did the strangest thing. She looked back at him in a way that was beyond the dream. Her eyes showed recognition, and her head turned at the slightest angle, as she did when devoting her attention to some small piece of the world.

It was to him, in the endless stair, that she looked. He felt her true presence and he tried to speak. His mouth was too dry, her radiance too insistent for his blind eyes, and he seemed to crumble before her.

He whispered her name: "Petra..."

Vandar's heart sank as she disappeared into the darkness. He stopped climbing the stairs, and his heart was pounding. He leaned back against the wall, his head spinning with fantasies of escape, his hand gripping the short sword like it had never known another function, his breath heavy and labored. He did not know. He could not tell time or space anymore. Weary, he wondered if the time had come to just lay down and surrender to his fate.

Tap - tap

He sank down to sit on the stair, facing down into the depths from which he had come, and it was then that he realized that he could see the silver blade of the short sword. It was faint, and he had thought it to be part of the dream, but he could see it surely enough. A faint reflection of light ran along the side of the blade, and when he touched it the shadow of his hand obscured it.

Light.

He turned around and looked up the stair. The taste of metal in his mouth was suddenly overpowering, and the thirst which overcame him now set him into a desperate strait. He shielded his eyes with a pale white hand, and emitted a grunt that might have been a word. He turned around and looked back into the darkness of the long stair. It descended into the earth like nothingness itself, like the stairway into the depths of a greedy soul.

Tap - tap - tap

Vandar climbed toward the light at the top of the stair, which now lit the way through the tunnel. He balanced himself against the wall as he climbed, and his sword hung in his right hand half-forgotten. He climbed and the thirst became stronger and stronger, and with each step he became surer that the weakness in his feet would overcome him completely. Now he took the steps two at a time, and the sound of the other feet on the stairs below suddenly dominated his attention: the thing that pursued him.

Vandar slowed as he approached the source of the light. Blinding. Not more than twenty steps up the last of the endless stair. He edged toward it, his eyes shielded by one hand, and he looked back into the darkness. He listened to the approach of the thing -- tap-tap-tap -- and he raised his sword up in readiness. Slowly, he backed his way up the stairs.

The pursuer's final footsteps came slowly. Tap. Tap. Tap. Vandar felt its presence below him on the stair, looking up from the shadows. He could not see it, but could only feel the eyes that lurked in the darkness, the coldness of its gaze. He stood now on the final step. The blazing sunlight engulfed him, and he looked down into the stair with a sense of glory and giddiness. He had escaped!

"To hell with you, beast!" Vandar shouted into the tunnel. He waited for a reply, but heard nothing. With a triumphant sense he went out into the daylight. He shielded his eyes from the sun and realized that although he could hardly stand the white light, it was in fact near dark. The sun hung low amid giant mountains, and he stood on a narrow path that traversed a steep slope. The opening was nothing more than a crack in the rock, and all around him stood great mountains topped with snow, and he stood high over a valley, on an inaccessible place without trees or shelter.

He looked back at the crack from which he had emerged and saw that a solitary figure stood there. It had the size and stance of his friend Koeno, and as soon as Vandar looked back the figure disappeared. The crack was once again an insignificant feature on the rocky slope.

Vandar called out. "Koeno!"

There was no reply. He was alone. His friends were dead. He knew that. Perhaps Koeno's ghost had been following Vandar all along. Perhaps Vandar had left him behind *prematurely*.

He stared at the opening where the stairs began. He would not go back. He could not face it.

In a valley far below ran a river that reflected silvery red with the light of the sinking sun. Vandar had to find his way down from his perch on the precipice. His thirst drove him mad as he futilely attempted to reach it before dark. When the path disappeared from underfoot, he felt his way along the steep and rocky slope. He sat among the rocks as the night came down in the mountains, and his thirst did not abate. He saw visions in the night, and he shivered in the mountain air.

He had reached Thane. The Wheel had turned.

Chapter Four: The Northlands

Only thin grass grew in the rocky soil of the long and narrow valley into which Vandar crept as the sun rose. A flat river ran along its length, entering at one end in a misty waterfall that blew about in the mountain winds, and exiting over a high falls at the far end. There too it fell on rocks far below, but these rocks lay in a deep impassable gorge. The valley itself harbored only tall, tough grasses that grew in gravelly soil, and similarly tough shrubs that kept close to the ground. It was not a long walk from either bank of the shallow river to the steep slopes of the valley's side, and not far up either of these that the slopes became walls, which rose up above the valley floor. The mountains ringed the sky in every direction, great jagged peaks covered at their heights with snow, occupying a sky that was so clear and blue that it defied all sense or memory. The island had always been shrouded in clouds and mists.

Vandar had come down into the valley, mad with thirst, his flesh whitened like that of a vampire, his mouth filled with the metallic taste of the water that seeped along the endless stair. He had slid and fallen, stumbled and crawled down from a place high on one of the walls of the valley. As he lay down by the river, his swollen stomach full to the breaking point with water, yet thirsty beyond belief, he looked up at the cliffs. He tried to remember which of the valley walls he had descended, and how he had managed to get down to the valley floor. He could not. He wondered if this had even been the valley that he saw from the entrance to the endless stair. Perhaps it was not. Perhaps he had looked down on one valley, then followed circuitous paths among the mountains and come down in a different place entirely.

It did not matter. He had not eaten in many days. The tall grass that grew in the valley was hardly nutritious, or hardly seemed to be, and he had eaten it straight off the stalk. It did not cure his weakness, and the thirst did not abate. His stomach was too full, and even laying by the side of the river was painfully awkward. His belly protruded so much that he had to lay on his side only--that way the ground helped to support his weight. But even that was not enough. He pulled himself up to his hands and knees and crawled back to the very edge of the river. He lay his face down in it and sucked the water down. The sensation of cold liquid flowing down his throat produced an indescribable bliss. It was a momentary relaxation of the thirst, that was all. But the bliss it produced was its own reward. Forgetting about the pain in his stomach, forgetting about the hunger, forgetting about all things except this salutary moment, Vandar drank all the cold riverwater that he could get down.

Nothing else moved in the valley, save the black birds that circled high overhead. Their nests dotted the high walls. The lost wanderer paused as he drank himself to death, and looked up in remembrance. He had seen their cousins in another world, where there was only the sea and the cliffs, and a lonely island. He had seen them high on the cliffs, circling and rising on winds where men could not go. Then he corrected himself. Men could go there. He had gone there. He was there now. It was in the middle of the day, but his aching body was too weak. He fell into a dream by the side of the winding river, and there he saw the island again. He was rising up from the bottom of the sea, and he was a waterman.

He had tentacles now, and his body was filled with poison. His arms hung by his sides, and the tentacles that sprouted at random points on his translucent body whirled and darted with their own hunting instincts. His jaw hung open, and seawater dripped from his lips. He thought and remembered the island, and he remembered his family. He came up from the water, lurching forward on unsteady feet, and he saw his father. He wanted to repudiate him, to denounce the cowardice of his name, to justify his flight with words that would win over all listeners, but all that emerged was a low growl. It came from the base of his throat with a putrid smell. It was the smell of death and poison. His father had brought with him fighters, whose long spears were the only weapon against the poisonous but slow waterman. Vandar knew this. He had used the spears himself, before the urge to glory led him back to Thane. He wanted to tell them about the mountains, the world, the thirst. He emitted once again a subhuman growl. Then the spears of the fighters jabbed at him. Pushed into his flesh. He cried out as he swung at them, too slow to keep them at bay--

He recognized them! Lazar was there, and so was Torjek. So was Koeno. All prodded at him with long spears. He would have cried out to them, but language had fallen beyond his grasp.

*   *   *

Vandar awoke to find a sword pressed against his throat. His arms were held down by strong hands, and shadows interrogated him. He choked and vomited clear water, and he could not speak. He heard laughter and shouting, and they picked him up by the arms. His belly sagged, the weight of the riverwater being enormous within him, and his feet dragged along the ground. He was surrounded by men who wore swords at their sides and carried spears and shields. A caravan of colorfully clad people with strange creatures that he took to be horses (from the tales he had heard as a child, with their bony legs and weirdly long faces) had at first stood by while his interrogation went on, and they now started to unpack and set up an encampment. The men put Vandar down in the dirt, where they stood around him and talked in a funny way--their words where similar to the Thanian he had known on the island, but their inflections seemed wrong, and the words were mispronounced.

Vandar's thirst was unquenchable, and he became desperate to drink from the river. He tried to stand, but weakness filled him. The men laughed. He cursed, and they laughed again. They asked him to repeat the curse--asked in their funny way. He did, and they laughed again. He asked where he was, and they would not answer. He asked to drink water.

"Tell us your name, traveler"

"Please, give me water."

"Your name. You have had plenty of water, by the look of you. Tell us your name now."

Vandar hesitated. He wondered whether they were minions of the traitor lords, whether their masters had blue skin and white hair, and ate the flesh of men. He wondered, but he could not resist them. One of them grabbed at the silver medallion of the Wheel. He could do nothing to resist as they removed it unhurriedly from around his neck. When they asked again he declared his name with all the force that he could muster:

"Harkess! I am Vandar Harkess! Now give me the water or kill me."

It came out as little more than a whisper. The men handed him a sack of water, and as he drank it down they talked between themselves. He did not hear or try to hear. He sucked down the water until the pain in his stomach became acute. Then he fell backwards onto the dirt. He vomited up water again, and coughed uncontrollably. He spat phlegm from his mouth and wiped it with his hand. Then he looked up at the armed men.

"I am dying anyway." He coughed again, and the thirst resumed with all its previous intensity.

One of the men knelt beside him. He pulled Vandar's short sword from its sheath and inspected it. He pointed at the Wheel that was inscribed at the base of the blade and showed it to the others. Then he said to Vandar, "You have been poisoned by the chokaro. It is in the earth in these parts, and kills by thirst. We are not slaves of the devils. We are free men. We will cure you."

Vandar looked up at him. The man's beard was red as red, and his long hair was tied back behind his head. His face was burned red from the sun, and his eyes were sky blue. Vandar looked up at the others. All were warriors, men of the hardy breed. Their weapons dangled at their sides. One by one they inspected the short sword with approving nods, and comments that Vandar could not hear. He passed in and out of dreams, and woke as he was being carried into a tent. He lay there for a while, sure that death was on him, then a woman sat down beside him and forced him to eat bites of a mashed-up plant. It was sweet and stringy, and although his stomach to full to the breaking point, he was glad to have it. He had not eaten for days. The feeling of something solid in his mouth produced its own satisfaction.

Then he passed back into the realm of sleep. His body felt warm beneath a blanket, and the pain in his stomach slipped away.

*   *   *

"We are the free-swords of Chetto Vorgos, or what remains of them. We are outlaws and free men, killers and thieves, but we live and die together. In these dreadful mountains we have lived and fought for twenty years. Now Chetto is gone, the Thanians are in the valleys, and we have come here to elude them. Since they killed him, they think they have us. But they are wrong. Look at this valley! When there is a place as good as this one, how could we ever be beaten? Eh? Look around you!"

The Left Hand let Vandar look, then he instantly discarded the pretense with a rueful laugh.

"The truth is that we cannot stay here long. There are ghosts in the higher ranges who would come for us at night, and this place has poison in the soil. Still, it makes for a useful retreat. We shall stay a week or so, then return to the valleys to join up with our cousins. There are at least a hundred free-sword bands in these mountains. We are friend to some. We have supplies hidden at a place down below."

The Left Hand looked Vandar in the eye. "Free-swords are never far from want. Nor from defeat. We would have it so to remain free men."

Vandar walked the perimeter of the tiny encampment with a man who called himself the Left Hand. He had knelt down and spoken to Vandar on the first day that the Free-swords came up to the valley, and his red beard shone in the cool and clear day. The wind in the valley was neverending, and the people of his band were wrapped in leather and furs.

Although Vandar was still weak, he walked with the Left Hand along the riverbank, and together they surveyed the encampment. The tents stood on poles, and beneath them the men and women of the Free-swords took their rest. A space had been cleared for a fire, but it was not yet lit. There were no trees anywhere in the high mountains, Vandar had been told. Although the free-swords had hidden supplies in the valley in the past (in preparation for times like this, when flight from the lower valleys could not be delayed for an instant), they had no reason to waste their firewood. This they had unearthed from its hiding place on the lower slope of the valley wall. They dug at it with sticks, and exulted when it was recovered. It lay piled in the center of the encampment, well guarded by the eyes of all.

Vandar counted forty men, twelve women, and five children among the Free-swords, and they took pride in their ragged freedom. They elected their leaders, and Chetto Vorgos had been one of the greatest. He had gathered together the free peoples of the mountains -- the Northlands, as the region was described to Vandar by the Left Hand and others -- and he had raided down into the green hill country of Thane itself. Chetto had been a good and devout man, whose love of liquor was equaled only by his love of the sword and the saddle. He was incorrigible, inviolable in memory, and all the people Vandar met recalled his days with bliss. That was when they had lived in a warm valley down in the lower range, and they had numbered five hundred fighting men in their village alone. When gathered together, the northern folk were invincible, they told Vandar. He saw the toughness of each of them, the meagerness of their means, and he was sure they were right.

They had sent an emissary to find their friends elsewhere in the high mountains, in the old hiding places, and they had posted sentries at the mouth to this high valley. They had taken with them a flock of sure-footed goats, their necks tied together by a long strand of hemp rope, for sustenance in the valley, and already there were plans to raid down into the lower valleys for more food. Their present sanctuary was hidden and watered, and for Vandar the high mountains that ringed the sky made it beautiful and holy, but it had that fatal flaw: no food, no trees, and no shelter. When the winter came, the snows would bury any who attempted to stay here.

Vandar lay in the tent of the Left Hand, still recovering from his poisoning, when a gathering of the men elected his host as their new leader. "I will follow!" each had vowed, and they held their sword-points together in the air. The women watched from their places at the fire, their voices silent. There was something of Petra in their silence, Vandar thought, and he wondered who they might elect if they had the chance.

He sat on a rock beside the shallow river and watched the men slaughter a goat for food. Before they killed it they drew a circle in the dirt, and they prayed out loud for courage and strength. Despite their strange dress and their bandit lives, despite the weird ways in which they spoke and the fact that he himself was born of exiles, they were still born of Thane, and kinsmen. Together the whole band prayed at a makeshift rock Wheel by the side of the river. Their voices rose to a single sustained note for the glory of the Wood.

He ate the strange sweet fruits that they gave him, and he rested. Soon he had regained his strength and could walk unaided. He sat beneath the blue sky and the mountains, beside the shallow river, and he felt the spirit of the Thanian land well up inside him. It had no voice, but the sense was enormous and moving. He bowed his head and then slipped to his knees. He pressed his forehead against the cold ground, and the roar of the spirit encompassed all.

*   *   *

The Left Hand brooded by the riverside. He had called Vandar to see him, and the two sat by themselves. He told Vandar that sentries had been posted along the route that led down to the lower valleys, the secret route known only to the free-swords. Two men had gone down into the valleys themselves to make contact with allies, but found only bands of enemies who fought one another. They saw Thanian formations too, but no friends.

The Left Hand's face had become a long grimace. "When the winter comes, we must have shelter. Or else my people will starve here. I cannot let that happen."

He has no choice but to lead them, Vandar thought. He wondered how the sense of responsibility must feel. How it would weigh down on a man. Then he remembered his last glimpses of his friends. He felt that he knew very much what the Left Hand felt.

"Let me help you," Vandar said. "You saved my life. Let me help you now. I will fight for you."

The Left Hand fixed his gaze on Vandar, and the calculations of his mind were visible on his face. "Then tell me about this island that you came from."

"It lays in the shadow of the great cliffs of the world. It has shelter and fishing and might make a good place for shelter if you could reach it. There is a tunnel somewhere up there. In the mountains." He waved his hand at the peaks that ringed the sky. "But at its end is a chamber of death, and the end of the world. My blood brothers died there. I will not lead you there too."

The Left Hand said nothing. He stared at Vandar for so long, with his eyes expressionless and cold, that Vandar wondered if he had decided to kill him. Then he spoke.

"I am just a man. Not like you. I was born a land-toiler. I will not die one. Perhaps this chamber of death can be overcome by strong men."

"It is the sea itself, friend. There is no way past it. That is why I am here. It took all my companions and very nearly took me too. I came through it and cannot ever go back."

"What is the sea?"

"The sea? It is the great body of water that lies beyond the edge of the world. It is cold and violent. It is filled with the spirits of the dead. Like the chamber at the end of the tunnel. The dead walk the bottom of the sea. They are monstrous. The sea itself is infinite. Beyond the island of the monastery there is nothing more forever."

"Yes." The Left Hand's eyes now took on a faraway air, and when Vandar spoke again the Left Hand did not reply. Then he murmured to himself, words that Vandar did not understand.

"My people are trapped on an island in that sea," Vandar said. "Beyond the edge of the world. Beyond the reach of the Wood."

"My people are trapped *here*," said The Left Hand. "I will not see them starve. The whole world is full of pain. Take me to the tunnel, and I will let you go where you may. But not before that. That is my price for your life."

"I cannot find it again."

"Then you shall be slave to me."

This is what Vandar became.

Chapter Five: The Forest Heresy

In the summer of the year before the year Zero, when the priest had settled into his small stone house and his books had found their places on the rickety shelf that his predecessor had built from logs found fallen in the wood, there came news that a hunting party from the fort had found an altar in the forest. They believed that it was an altar of the Old Believers, the heretical sect that still worshiped in these parts, and of which the priest had heard rumors and given condemnatory sermons.

A circle of eight stones, with a smooth round stone at the center. The trappings of the Old Belief were widely known among the devout, for every mother told her children of the Old Believers and their wickedness, that they preferred unruly children to good ones, and that they would come in the night, or in the day when no one else would see them, to steal them away for sacrifice in the center of their round altar, the Wheel. The priest and the Sheriff traveled into the hills to investigate. One of the hunters led them through the cool forest which made the priest wish that he had brought a heavier robe, to a bright open field atop a low hill. To the north lay the everpresent mountains, and to the south Scoms and the rest of Thane.

Along the edge of the field they found it: a circle of eight stones polished smooth and glassy, and in the center a single round rock with a flat top and jagged lines inset at strange angles. The priest shuddered when he saw it, because it was like a picture straight from the seminary, and he stood by the edge of the Wheel and looked into the forest. The Old Believers worshiped a powerful demon in the earth, the priest knew, which granted them strange powers. He had been told once that they could make themselves invisible and that they could fly like birds. Could they see him now, he wondered. Could they read into his heart? Richard and his men held back from the altar, their attention on all the directions from which ghouls might leap. For their cruelty, the priest saw, they were scared and little men.

The priest stepped across the outer ring of stones and into the Wheel itself. He smiled when Richard called for him to come back, and although he found himself afraid, the fear did not outweigh his curiosity. Here was a genuine altar of the Old Belief. It hardly looked old or long unused, although the grass had grown in around the rocks the way that it does when something sits in one place for long. He knelt and looked at the hub, the flat rock with the jagged lines. A small part of him wanted to touch it, to feel the cool rock with his own finger, but curiosity alone was not enough to make him do that. No. He had seen enough. He stepped back out of the circle with glances over his shoulder, and headed back toward the fearful Sheriff and his men. They hurried him to walk faster, and when the party left the clearing they went briskly back toward the town. They looked fearfully at the shadows in the wood, and the noises of the owls and the birds became weird songs to their ears.

*   *   *

In the fort of the Lord Istan Famm, past the muddy and manure-filled central yard, a passage through a thick door led to the great room. Here Famm conducted his business and took his meals, and here the priest confirmed the hunters' finding. The Lord Famm watched the priest draw out with his hands in the air a crude diagram of the altar.

"Stupid dogs!" Famm nailed a fist into the arm of his thick and darkly lacquered chair. "I knew they still clung to it. Dreamers all, that's the *land-toiler* for you. Show them the world, show them the real world, and they will stupidly till their fields and listen to their witches. Damn!"

"I shall issue a report to Riadom, my lord," said the priest. "They shall instruct us as to proper steps. I suppose that they will send investigators to search the village itself. They have men, you know, who can sense the presence of an Old Believer. They are learned in the ways of demonic worshop in places where it persists across the empire."

"Yes yes," Famm said. "I understand that the Church keeps itself apprised of all such things. But we must act today. Tonight. I'll not have the heretics loose. What did they teach you in your schools, priest? Soft ways, eh? The ways of theology and contemplation I'll wager. Well here in the mountain district we must not be soft. Bandits raid from the mountains. We live by the rain and the sun, and when God decides, our crops fail. *I* protect the land-toiler from all these things. *I* catch the bandits who rob them and rape their women, and when they starve *I* open my stores to feed them. They are ingrates who do not care what I do for them. No, oh no. They secretly worship a demon in the earth. They persist in this heresy, and I shall not tolerate it. Nor shall I allow soft-hearted mercy to undermine me. You are new, and you will learn the truth of what I say. I will *not* appeal to Riadom. I will solve this puzzle with whips and fire."

"Lord Famm, I think I have a suggestion for you," the priest said quietly. "I acknowledge the truth of what you say. I am new and perhaps soft to your ways, but I am learning.

"I hope you might find some use in what they did teach me in the south. Although I am admittedly a man of books, I would suspect that the sort of action you intend to take against the land-toilers would be quite disruptive to the cultivation of the fields, the milking of the cows, and the other tasks of theirs that enrich you and provide you the wealth that you have accrued.

Perhaps there is another way for us to accomplish our goal."

Famm nodded slowly. "What do you propose?"

"Demon worship was the quite common in the lifetime of the Hyacinth. The various demonic creatures have common characteristics that may play to our advantage as men of faith and as stern investigators. First of these is sacrifice. Demons demand blood. These Old Believers must soon gather at the altar to make a sacrifice, and your men can catch them there if we are watchful. Then we are obligated to show mercy. We must offer those that we capture a chance to refute the Old Belief and join us. Some will surely refuse. They will cling to their demon. We will burn them on stakes if you like, or we can hang them before the fort. They are damned already."

Strong emotions filled the priest. Anger. Fear.

* * *

When he left the fort of Lord Famm all things were different. The day itself, although still warm and friendly, was now nothing more than the prologue to the purging of the Old Believers. It was the priest's duty to battle the Old Belief; it was his nature to protect the innocent. He made his way down the hill and past the hanging tree, and on the dusty road to the village he looked out across the fields. Green lines of corn slowly surged toward the sun, and the wheat fields fluttered lazily with the softest breeze. Among the crops, which were all the property of Istan Famm, the land-toilers went about their labors. They carried water or hay for the horses, dug ditches where the overseers had determined that ditches were needed, and watched over the sheep and cattle. They were all blind to the future as the priest now knew it would unfold. Lord Famm and his men would come at night, and just ahead, where the first huts of the village began, they would push the land-toilers away from their homes while the searches got underway. They would beat them and pay for betrayals, and although the priest brooked no kindness to heretics himself, and could find in his heart mercy but barely forgiveness, he could not look at the land-toilers the way that he had the day before, or even the hour before. Swords and whips and fire, these would be Famm's tools, and surely Richard would not hesitate to err on the side of killing too many.

It would be his commandment.

Terror would be their weapon, and the priest would stand beside them. He would sanction Famm's death sentences, and urge the accused to confess so that they might die quickly. He hoped he had the fortitude for what might happen to those who refused. Their ends would come slowly and with great pain, he was sure. They would cremate the dead at dawn, in the tradition of the True Belief, when God's light bathed the world in the new day. Is this really what the Hyacinth had wanted?

The priest would be there, but he could not stand the thought. Yes, it was his duty to fight the Old Belief, but he was a man of books and a man of kindness. For him the greatest power of the True Belief was in its infinite mercy and the good people who made their lives in its service. They believe in God's light and they live by the Hyacinth's code. I try to do the same, he thought. This made all the evils of the empire -- and, in truth, no other word could describe them -- bearable. So why would the forest heretics who called themselves Old Believers worship a demon?

*   *   *

It was a book of the Old Belief, *Orlov's Guide for Wary Churchmen*, that led the priest to doubt his own judgment. This thin parchment volume, with its stink of age and mold, had lain in the bottom of his chest since before his departure from Riadom. He read it though the day in his shuttered house by the orange glow of a pigfat candle, and it enumerated the sins of the Old Believers: sacrifices in the earth, a demonic presence that craved blood. These things he saw in it with a mixture of revulsion and curiosity. What power was there in the wood that his own faith could not dispel? What force could the Old Belief command that the True Belief, the heart of the church and the center of the priest's whole life, could not? The priest had made up his mind to see for himself.

He made his way up from the village, back along the trails that he had followed only that morning with Richard and the hunter. He left behind him the cooking fires and the naked children, left behind the straw roofs and the pigs, the chickens and the sheep. He climbed the steep trails and found himself descending within sight of the northern mountains, the jagged peaks and the snowy passes, the great impassable wall between Thane and the end of the world, which drew the criminals and deserters, the runaway land-toilers of the Thanian provinces. This was the reason for Famm's harshness. Were he to loosen his grip on his people, and they were by law quite literally his people, that they too might flee for the northern waste.

The priest came upon the open field, and stopped well short. He lurked in the shadows of the forest for a time, and doubts began to consume him. He had lapsed again in judgment, his conscience reminded, in even coming to this place. The True Belief was a wall that could protect him from all things, or from most, and it certainly could protect against the temptation of curiosity, if only he would let it. He wrapped himself tightly in his robe, and stood quite still. Out across the field, the Wheel beckoned. He had stood in it only this morning, and had kept himself from touching the smooth stone. Was that restraint to avoid scaring Richard, or was it to avoid the greater temptation?

The Old Belief. His heart beat quickly, and as he recited to himself a thousand false reasons for legitimately coming to this place, he knew that he had never been suited to this frontier post. He was a man of thinking, a man of study, and he reviled his sinful heart.

The priest had loved, and he had seen fornicators run through the streets of Riadom. He had walked in sunny fields, and he had seen failed crops withered and dry. He had dreamed, and he had seen the darkest hours of the night when sleep would not come and guilt poured through him. He was a man, although consecrated to God, and in him all the failings of the flesh lurked. They subverted and tempted, whether in the form of fury at a wrongly hanged man, or lust at the view of a young strong land-toiler woman (that path he always denied himself, always). He tried always to remain loyal and true to the Church and to himself, and to the rightful lords of Thane. But temptation lapped at his feet, a gentle bath of sin, and he was not as strong as he wished he could be.

He stood like a statue, his robe drawn around him to keep out the chill as the sun set. *He should not have come here.* If they were out there, if the Old Belief truly gave its adherents powers that he had never seen in the Church, if they moved invisibly through the wood, could they see him now? He felt that they might. But he also felt that he would surely sense them, as a man of the Church himself, and he felt nothing. No eyes, no prying consciousness within reach, no lurking spirits. As light and shadow faded into a single grey fabric, as the sun's eyes slipped shut, he stepped out into the clearing with a vow that he would but touch the hubstone, as he had wanted to do earlier. Although this in itself constituted a submission to temptation, his thinking had become distorted and unclear. He sought to justify himself, but he could not. With every step toward the circle of stones, he knew that he was stained.

He stepped within the circle as he might have touched a woman. His heart seemed near to exploding, and he felt fully and dreadfully alive. The stars had begun to appear, and moon with them, and he could see the hubstone before him, set firmly in the grassy ground, its markings invisible in the grey light.

As he knelt slowly and reached out his right hand to touch it, and only to touch it once, a shape appeared before him. It wove itself of the grey moonlight, and stood atop one of the wheelstones that comprised the outer edge of the circle. He felt sweat appear all over his body, and a wave of nervous energy swept through him. It was a figure of a man, or a woman, or the night itself, and as he stared at it, his hand frozen in its reach toward the hubstone, it spoke to him.

"Tare," it said. That was his given name. "I offer you courage."

This was the Old Belief.

Intoxicated and drenched with the sinfulness of the moment, the priest found himself unable to say or do what he had known all his life was right. Beneath his black robes and his woolen cap, beneath all the years of careful learning, and beneath even his thrashed-in fealty to the True Belief in defiance of all else, the priest was less a priest than a man. And here, speaking to him and him alone, was the ancient power of the Old Belief.

"I accept," he said.

They appeared at that instant, woven of the night and seated all around him on the wheelstones. Weird and vaguely discernible faces of men and women, haunting eyes that stared through his priestly adornments and saw into the soul that he had exposed. They had, somehow, been there all along. And now they sang.

The music was not like music at all. There were no words and no melody, no meaning to the ears, but all their voices coalesced into a single sustained tone that penetrated the priest and seemed greater than itself. It hummed, and his bones hummed with it. He was inside it with them, with the spirits of the Old Belief, and it was as if his life had ended and a new one had begun. He could never be the same person again.

The message of the voices was this: "Did you think that they were *always* your masters?"

Pain shot through his body. At first it appeared as aches in his joints, then enveloped him fully. In his toes and fingers, in his knees and his chest, the pain was extraordinary and violent. He felt as if he were coming apart, as if the music and the singers were killing him for his transgressions, and he almost would have welcomed such an end, having seen them and their power in all its weird truth, and he cried out because he could not control himself. The pain filled his jaw and his teeth, and it burned and ached and stung him, and his cries became hoarse and primitive, and somehow in the cloud of the pain, in the shroud laid over him by the singers and the song, he realized that he was not dying at all.

He was *growing*. His body convulsed with pain, burst out of his garments and grew. His boots peeled away to free his feet. His tunic burst at the seams, and his woolen cap slid from his massive head. The black robe itself split at the neck and down the back seam. From within, massive new muscles took shape on his growing frame. They were not what they had been before, the muscles of a priest whose work was largely done with a book or quill. These were the muscles of war.

Then visions emerged from the night itself. He saw into the past, onto a field on which two armies stood. It came in flashes and bursts, in sight and in thoughts that he could not have thought himself. It came from *them*, from the singers, and as the priest cried out with the pain of his transformation, he saw a past that he had never known. One army was that of the Masters. Moving in rapid precision. Golden shields. Long bright swords. And the other was an army of men. *Thanians*. He knew which one was king and which were the lords. He knew the lords by name: Firo, Harkess, Basala, Exus, Janara, Vorgos. Over their heads fluttered prayer flags, strange banners. This was the past, filled with absurdities. Thanian lords. A free Thanian army standing against the Masters. Raising their swords against an enemy that was innumerable, that commanded the field, that converged on them from all sides when they did not see. He saw the killing frenzy, the confusion on the field. The banners of the noble houses swarmed by the Masters. Pulled down. Engulfed.

At that moment he finally truly *saw*. This was more than the sight lent by eyes and by light. He saw with his whole mind a presence that existed through himself, through the land, through the trees and the earth. The hum of the singers captured a churning, humming life-force greater than all the prayers and faith and self-abnegation of all his years of schooling, greater and more real than any of the resonant tales of the Hyacinth, greater than anything he might have felt in the brightest and most sanctified dawnlight ceremonies. The presence filled him with what he knew were its own wild emotions: anger, anger, anger. He recognized this for a moment as the sin that it was, but only for an instant, because he forgot himself and his care and his temperance and his mercy and all his meticulous learnings. The pure essence of the anger absorbed him. Its fury became his own. His denial and his faith fell away and in that same instant he welcomed some piece of the thing into him.

The priest saw this, and he saw more.

Chapter Six: The Witness

The priest saw more.

Blue hands wielding spears and clubs. Beating on the heads of men and boys. Screaming and choking on the dust, the blood, the fear. Their golden shields were unstoppable, their swords irresistible. They slashed at the fighters, whose blood fed the field. They gutted the shieldboys, hanged them upside down from their black banners, took heads for their trophies.

Here are your Masters for you... came the message of the singers.

The priest cried out, seeing it now. He could not turn away, could not stop the vision. He floated over the field, and the cruel acts multiplied everywhere he looked. "Renounce your Wood!" the Masters commanded those who had thrown down their weapons. Those who refused paid dearly. Here a group of blue-skinned Masters stretched a man out on the ground, and killed him with swords while he screamed and struggled. There the lords of Thane were hacked to death by slaves of the Masters, their heads and limbs separated from their bodies and heaped by the river.

The blind king of Thane, Carrillon, whose advisors described the battle to him, whose position on a hill-top behind his army was the last surrounded and captured when he himself refused to run, was now set upon by his captors. He would not renounce the Wood. They stripped him of his crown and garments, and on the field beheaded him under the watchful eye of the sun itself. And God, the priest reminded himself, his mind reeling with the horror of the sight. The light of day shone on these acts: this was God's light as the Hyacinth taught.

Why did we not know?

And the priest floated in the air as no man had, and he witnessed the worst of all days. The Masters walked the earth over the bodies of Thanian men. They offered freedom in return for renouncing the Wood and taking up the True Belief. Those who agreed became their accomplices. They defiled their comrades and took their heads, and they forced them to parade in the shorn skins of their brothers. The Masters forced one man to murder another, and forced then another to gut the killer. Then all were set upon by the Masters themselves and their slaves, and tortured and their throats were cut from ear to ear. The dying were numberless on the field. The new converts cried, their bloody hands soaked too with tears.

Where was God's light now?

The priest cried out, floating on the air, his arms and legs useless instruments. He looked to God in heaven and cursed his own fate: to witness these acts and be powerless, to be *weak*.

He had always been weak, and had always borne it as a given. He had shunned the stronger brothers and kept to himself, in the library, in the monastic towers that overlooked the dusty Thanian capital at Riadom. All the flesh and its horrors he had kept far from himself, and here were the worst crimes committed right before him. He did not know them by name, the victims, but they were men like himself, and boys, whose families and blood were like his own. Thanian. Of this land. Conquered and enslaved.

Or killed, as all these men were when they refused to renounce the Wood. *All of them.* Slowly and with a murderous joy, with a parading power and perverse crimes. The captured Thanians saw this, and their fates were sealed.

The priest saw this, and he saw more. He saw an injured Thanian man looking directly at him as he awaited the attention of his captors. The man sat in an open space with hundreds of others, his bloody tunic hanging from his body, and his eyes dead and knowing. He stared up into the air at the priest, and he was not the only one. Others among the Thanians looked to him. And they called out: "See what these devils do to us! Do you? They will kill us all!"

He could say nothing. The doomed men called to him. "Tell the world what they do to us! Tell the people how we died at Coormo!"

Devils took note of his presence, and they gathered below him. The priest wanted to give the Thanian men a message, but his voice was clogged with horror. He could only look at them and know their fate, and his mouth moved but he could say nothing. Then the daylight began to fade around him and he knew that the vision was coming to an end. He was being taken away, and his message went with him. Even as they faded from his vision he tried to tell them.

I am your witness.

I shall be your voice.

*   *   *

It was night again, in a dark clearing in the strange northern lands, and the priest's body thrummed with pain. He lay on the grass in the center of the Wheel, rolling his head from right to left and crying out uncontrollably. He lifted his hands up to his hand, huge bearlike things that they had become, pulsing and stinging with pain, and growing more. He smashed a fist down on the ground beside him.

Coormo. The word had been an obscene whisper among the students. None knew its meaning.

Until now.

His eyes throbbed, but he opened them. His hands stung, but he put them down on the grass to balance himself. His legs similarly throbbed, having become very much like the trunks of trees, and his ribs and guts ached and burned, but he pulled himself up to a sitting position there in the night, and his head spun but he tried to think.

Think!

He could scarcely create a sensible train of words in his head. When the dawn came he knew that he had changed forever. So alone. Solitary in his knowledge, in what he had seen, in his pain. He sat in the clearing and he knew that he could not ever rest. He got to his feet and gathered up the clothes that he had worn. They were ripped and shredded, and he wrapped the remains of his priestly robes around himself as a loincloth. His huge hands were difficult to manipulate, but he tied the ends into a knot.

His body still hurt, but not with anywhere near the intensity that of the pain that had gone on before, during the visions, while he grew. He now stood several heads taller than he had ever been. He looked down at his body. Muscles rippled beneath his skin, and his arms and legs seemed to fill with vitality and power. And rage. He could not shake from his mind the pictures of what he had seen. What shame in defeat, what shame. But the shame of that was dwarfed by the treachery of the lords and the Church. He had never suspected the magnitude of the lie, or his own involvement, his own betrayal...

The Masters had not come bearing wisdom, but had instead inflicted unspeakable cruelty. Thanians had not gathered to the True Belief. Not as the Church taught. He had seen them. *He knew.* He knew the truth.

The rage, the fury. The pain he had seen. It could not be contained. He shook his fists and his huge legs carried him into the center of the clearing. He did not look or care where he walked, he thought only of the poor victims, the shame, the shame. He waved his arms around and lost his balance on the new feet. He fell down to the grass and beat it with his fist. Again and again, slamming it into the cold dirt, pounding the grass down, making a hole in the black earth, a place to put his rage.

"Whore's sons! You used me! You lied to me! Ah God help me! You lied! You *lied*!"

His charges degenerated from words to a long dark howl. He beat the earth with his fist, beat it and beat it and beat it. He beat it down. He would do the same to them. He would beat them down. He alone had seen the truth. He who had been Tare, whose identity had been *given* by the false Church, and who had given himself to it in turn. He would throw that name away.

The Old Belief was not just a forest heresy. No, the Wood had power. It had selected him and shown him these things. It had made *him* the witness at Coormo. Once it had reigned across all of Thane. The Masters and the Church had destroyed it with the cruelest of means. But now! Now there would be a reckoning.

Now the Wood had awoken. Its power needed no proof.

He would serve the Wood as a warrior.

In the darkest hours of the night, he sat quietly in the clearing. Clarity. This he sought and it came to him. He would no longer be Tare, for that was a slave's name. He was a free man, and alone. He chose a name that marked him uniquely: The Witness. It fitted him now, and he would die with it.

Chapter Seven: Hammer and Sword (1)

The giant hurtled through the dark forest as the sun rose over the enslaved land of Thane. The hills were the same as they had been the day before, but everything had changed. He knew the Masters for what they were. And he knew the Thanians too: a people who had once been free.

But what of the Church that called itself the True Belief?

The name was a lie. The hands behind it were the hands of the conquerors. All the lords and the masters of Thane, all those who called themselves Thanian warriors, all the wielders of power in this poor land, all were puppets of the true masters. That was the same on this morning as it was on any other: true and irrefutable. The pleading captives at Coormo returned to him again and again. Their hopeless faces, their cries. Thane was as much a slave today as yesterday.

Only *he* had changed, only the one who had been Tare. *But what he had seen.* He could not bear the weight. What mute God would make him witness such horrors and explain nothing. Why? To what end did he see the past?

Perhaps there was no purpose. Like the academies of the Church and the thousand tiny rituals he had learned as a boy, like the chants and the uniforms and the long days of prayer. What purpose did those things have in a false religion? Perhaps the whole world was just as random and idiotic, just as pointless. That would make every life and death nothing at all, and the pain of the Coormo captives would be nothing at all, and every conviction or dream or hope would also be nothing. The whole world would be nothing, and The Witness himself would be nothing, and the lives of the poor would be nothing. They would be dust, and their pain and slavery would be a matter of no more interest or importance than the size of the rocks in the trail that led back to the village of Scoms.

The giant Witness stopped in the trail. He knelt down and picked up one of the rocks. It was grey and did not weigh very much. It was about the size of his thumbnail, and he gripped it in his fist. How much more inconsequential could anything be? A rock in a trail, to be stepped on and forgotten. But it was also more than that. It had come from somewhere, and perhaps it had been left here on purpose by someone who was long since gone, like the rocks that composed the Wheel, the pattern of which could go unseen by anyone unversed in the meanings of the Old Belief. Perhaps this grey rock had its own secret purpose. It might be thrown at an enemy, or put in a sack with hundreds of other rocks to make a weight, or used to plug a hole in the wall of a hut in the village. It might have a thousand uses, all unseen at first glance.

The Witness realized that the rituals of the false Church also had their own unseen use: to perpetuate the slavery of the faithful. Every prayer, every book, every chant and every fast had as their penultimate aim the domination of the people by those who had sold themselves to the conquerors. Everything. Even the good, even the kindness and charity, even the concern for the soul. All of it came from the same black goal: domination and slavery by control of the soul.

"Obey your betters"... How many times had he himself preached to land-toilers about how they should never strive for a greater lot in life? How many times had he quelled them? The True Belief exalted slavery and the blue flesh not because it was holy, but because it was convenient for the Masters.

Had the Hyacinth ever really lived? If she had, the meaning of her life and her words had been lost. The shapers of the True Belief had twisted her words -- once treasured and holy to a man called Tare -- to make them the base principles of slavery: Obey your betters. Pray for greater faith. Keep hope.

The Witness bowed his head and prayed for strength. How could he have been a part of it? How could he *now* bring it to an end? He placed the rock back in its spot on the trail and stood up again.

If all things had a purpose, perhaps that rock's purpose had been to rest in this place, on this trail, until a certain angry man picked it up. Perhaps its purpose was to be reflected upon, to change everything, and then to wait for the end of the world. The Witness wondered this as he stood over the rock for a final moment, and then he continued on the trail to Scoms. He had a purpose, and all things had purpose, and his soul hummed like a bell.

*   *   *

The Witness came down from the hills. The morning light shone on the forest and the fields. He hid at the edge of the fields and peered out toward the village of Scoms and the fort of Lord Famm. Columns of smoke trailed up into the air from cooking fires in the village, and the cows and sheep and goats wandered about the shacks and huts. The smell of the village came on a waft of air, and he thought of the hanged thief Tallet. From the edge of the forest he watched the last moments of the old days of slavery in Thane.

Land-toiler men and women worked the fields. On their knees, they worked at the ground with small implements, their whole bodies dirty and lean from the job. Out across the field he saw that one of the Richard's men, on horseback, watched over the land-toilers. Behind him, the fort of Lord Famm rose up from the flat fields, and the smoke that came from within it billowed and swirled. The horseman looked lazy and nearly asleep in the morning sun. The Witness knew his dull eyes, his cruel reputation. What amount of the Devils' empire in Thane rested on his shoulders? The Witness saw images in his mind's eye that he could not dismiss as imaginings: the horseman raping a land-toiler girl, stealing tiny valuables from the village elders, and delivering them to his master in the fort. He saw the horseman in the woods, hunting down the Old Believers with a sword, cutting at old women from horseback as they fled hopelessly, already seen, easily identified if they survived to return to the village.

The Witness saw such *things*.

He had lurked behind a tree on the field's edge, but now he stood up. He had business with the horseman and the horseman's master. He had business with all the traitors and thieves, and these would be the first.

"People! I come to free you! People of Scoms!" The Witness shouted as he came out onto the field. "The Wood has shown me the truth! We must rise today!"

He was a towering man now, whose muscles rippled and who stood several heads higher than the tallest normal man. He was a giant in every sense, and his long black hair and black beard flowed with the breeze. He was barefoot and wore only the rags of his priestly vestments as a loincloth. He called out to the scattered land-toilers in the field and to the horseman, who now looked at him and seemed quite awake. The land-toilers, fearful, backed away from him. Even those farthest across the fields seemed to move away from him. The closest ran.

"I was your priest! Do not run! You know me! I was your priest but I have been to the hills! I saw the Wheel! I have come back for you! I am your Witness!"

They did not listen to him.

The Witness marched toward the horseman, clenching his great hands into blocklike fists. The horse bucked and kicked. Backed off fearfully as the horseman drew his sword. Protecting the villagers as they ran.

"Rider!" The Witness said. "I know you. Will you fight me? Do you have a drop of courage in you?"

The horseman wheeled his mount around and set off across the field. He looked back over his shoulder as he rode. The Witness shouted out to the running land-toilers, but they would not listen. He walked the old familiar path from the field into the village, and found the place shut up and fearful. Chickens and goats wandered about lazily, and did not shy away from him. It was only the people who hid, and he understood their reasons. They were afraid, and he might once have been afraid himself.

He tried to explain to them.

"People of Scoms, I was once your priest. But now the Wood has shown me things I did not know. *You* know. Many of you. You are its children. You are Old Believers, are you not? Now I have joined you. The Wood has made me its warrior. It has shown me that we are not animals. We were free once! We stood and fought like men against the Masters. We were not always their dogs. Nor dogs to men like Richard! Or Lord Famm! I will not be a slave anymore! To no one!"

He looked toward the old stone house that had been his. It lay at the edge of the village. Clustered all around him were the tiny shacks, the windowless huts, the dark and cold places where the land-toilers made their homes.

"I touched the Wheel!" He told the hidden listeners. "I have changed! I embrace the Old Belief--"

Those were the words of the heretic. With them he sealed his fate. Any who heard him might testify against him before the Judges at Riadom, or before Lord Famm and his executioners. The Witness did not care. He repeated them once softly, then shouted them as loud as he could:

"I embrace the Old Belief!"

They would come for him. But first he would share what he knew. He stood in the middle of the village and asked the villagers to come out. To listen to him. He swore that he would exculpate them of blame. He would die alone if he had to. But first he wanted to share with them.

The Wood.

The altar and its song.

What strength the Wood had put into him.

And they came out to listen. One by one. First it was the younger men, who ignored the pleadings of their elders. Their wives, who put down their children and came out into the dusty road, who lingered near the trees within earshot, who let themselves be seen. Soon they were joined by those very elders, by their wives. The Witness knew that others remained hidden. Fearful. He feared for them too and did not take offense.

"We have only the Wood to protect us," he told them when he saw the riders approaching from the fort. "Otherwise we must fight."

The villagers said nothing. They melted away as the Sheriff and a half dozen of his men entered the village. They carried lances and swords and flaming torches. The Witness stood alone in the street. He thought for a moment that this might be the end. He had made his peace with the spirits of the Wood. For this they would burn him. The grey skies were silent and the Wood was far off across the field. He had been a priest once. He had touched the Wheel.

Richard and his men confronted The Witness. Surrounded him in the center of the village. They kept back away from him. He turned in a circle. Staring at their eyes. These were the same criminals who had hanged the thief. In their glorified slave garb. With their swords.

"Where have you come from, giant? Did the heretics summon you?" Richard demanded to know.

"I was the priest here, Richard. No one summoned me. Call me the Witness. That is my name now. I shall not move for I have seen the truth. I shall not rest until Thane is free."

"Really?" Richard looked around for the villagers. Peering from their shacks. "Do you stand with him, toilers? Or does he stand alone?"

Then without warning he kicked at his horse and lurched forward and jabbed at the Witness with his long lance. The Witness reflexively raised his left hand to defend himself and the point pierced it slightly. Richard snarled and plucked the point away. Blood leaked from it, but the pain was no worse than the pain of his transformation. In fact it was not too bad. It distracted but did not incapacitate.

He stepped backward. The horsemen behind him moved back too. Richard came after him again. Jabbed at him. The Witness retreated again. He had no weapon, and Richard followed him like a cat. The lance came after him again and he dodged it. Richard cursed him and jabbed again. This time it struck him solidly in the thigh. The Witness cried out and Richard plucked the lance free.

"Now get on your knees, Churchman! They might have made you bigger, but I think this will still fit you!"

One of the horsemen unrolled a rope. On its end was a noose. The Witness cried out and lunged backward between two surprised horsemen, who pulled their horses aside instead of striking him. He retreated and Richard followed him, jabbing at him with the insurmountable lance. Richard kept his horse at a walk. Keeping pace with the Witness, who struggled on his knees. The other horsemen kept pace with him too. The Witness waved off the lance again and again with his bloody left hand.

Well-practiced hands now flung the rope and ensnared him by the neck. The noose closed tightly. Choking him. The lance struck him again. This time it was a deeper wound. In the ribs. He cried out. Took the rope by one hand. Struggling to stand. Jerked it out of the rider's hands. Richard closed in again on him. The bloody point of the lance just missing him.

He backed up again, not seeing where he went.

Dodged the lance again--

Punched through a wall--

And fell into the smithy's shop. Collapsing the wall into splinters and boards beneath him. He opened his eyes. The smith's fire glowed red in the brazier beside him. The smith's tool lay all about the dirt floor. The Witness sat up, his wounds almost forgotten, glowering at the riders who looked down from their mounts at him through the hole in the broken wall. Richard now began to dismount.

The Witness reached across the floor. The tools lay scattered. He took the largest hammer and felt its weight in his hands. It felt good. It felt strong.

The blacksmith's shop was one of the wealthiest in the village. It was covered by a wooden roof, though which the stone chimney protruded, and wooden walls on three sides. One of these walls had crumbled beneath him. The brazier stood in the center of the shop. The Witness now stood up beside the brazier. He emerged from the smithy and Richard was there to challenge him with his sword drawn. The look on Richard's face as his looked *up* at the giant betrayed his fatal surprise. The Witness slung the hammer in a great and sudden arc that ended on one side of Richard's head. Blood and brains sprayed out from the place of impact and Richard fell dead on the spot.

The Witness looked down at the dead man at his feet. A cockeyed expression marred his face. Blood leaked from his eyes.

The other horsemen backed off with curses.

The Witness stepped over the body of Richard. The hammer clenched in one fist. "Will you run now, you cowards? Will you?"

"What whore birthed you, giant?" One of the riders shouted. "You should have been strangled."

"I won't be a slave!"

"You're a fool!" The rider started down the path at full speed. Lifted his sword to strike. Clumps of mud flew up behind him. His fellows joined behind him uncertainly. When the first horse was a few steps away the Witness started toward it with a great arrogant step. The hammer swung in a wide horizontal arc. And brained the horse. It dropped into the dirt with its rider falling hard with surprise. The rider held his sword over himself protectively, struggling to free himself from beneath the horse. The Witness stood over him and landed a single blow that broke the sword and the arm that held it. The hammer landed with full force on the center of the man's chest. With a final blow to the head the Witness killed him.

Then he looked up at the other riders.

They had stopped short in their charge. Confronting the giant with two of their number dead already. He could see that these were not men who often found a fight. He challenged them, but they backed off from him, and with some indecision they retreated from the village. He walked out to the edge of the village as they sped back to the fort. Watching them fly along the rutted path between the fields.

What had he now set into motion? He could not let it stop.

Back in the center of the village the toilers gathered. He told them that the age of miracles had now begun. That these were only the first to die. That the people would be free. One by one the men of the village took up their scythes and clubs. They gathered to him.

"We are all Old Believers," they told him. "We have waited for you, Witness. The spirits told us you would come. They visit us in our huts at night. They permeate the land. Yes, we will fight with you. The whole land is ready."

And with that they set out to war. The Witness raced at the head of them. Waving the hammer over his head. Urging them forward. The visions burned in him, the horror of the field of Coormo, the screaming captives. The monstrousness.

Chapter Eight: Hammer and Sword (2)

The Witness pulled the hammer back from the splintered and beaten gate of the fort of Lord Famm. It did not come easily, having lodged firmly in its steel-reinforced oaken panels, but he pulled it out and peered into the hole that he had created. He saw men with swords, some half-dressed in armor and mail, shouting and running about in confusion. He saw the panic, the fear among the defenders, and then he saw one of them peer back at him. The peerer's eye was blue and curious. The Witness stepped back in surprise.

In an instant he swung the hammer back at the gate, and blasted another hole in the splintering barrier. The armed men of the village, who gathered all around him on the slope below the grey fort and whose own weapons included clubs, torches, scythes, and their own small knives, cheered once again. They cheered every blow. Finally the gate broke open. Parts of it fell to the left and parts fell to the right, and the remains that hung from the huge iron hinges were no barrier at all. All around The Witness a roar went up from the men, and he himself led the charge into the inner yard of the fort. This dusty enclosure, where chickens and pigs often wandered about, was surrounded by the grey walls and inner buildings of the fort. There was the horse stall, the barracks, the well, and the more ornate house of the Lord Famm, which was no less dusty than the rest of the fort.

The Witness pushed aside the first of the dismounted horsemen who attacked him as he entered the inner yard of the fort. The man, who wore a steel helmet and a dark tunic, had been waiting beside the gate with his sword ready, but he had not struck quickly enough. Perhaps the sight of the giant was too much for him, perhaps he had seen the hammer's short work in the village and knew that his own death was imminent. The Witness pushed him down with a great sweep of the hand, while holding the hammer in the other hand, and his poorly armed villagers engaged Lord Famm's mercenaries. Famm's men were skilled with swords and axes, and the villagers of Scoms were not fighters. The first to fall was an older man whose youngest son had fled to the mountains and whose daughters had nine children between them. The Witness saw him lunge at a swordsman with a large club for his weapon, only to be sidestepped and cut down. Next came one of Famm's men: his sword was wrested away from him and the villagers hacked wildly at him as he tried to shield himself. It seemed to the Witness that Famm's men might beat the villagers: they fought with more skill, with better weapons, and at least equal bravery.

That would have been the old story. The villagers would have been driven off even if they had somehow come to the fort (which they would not have done) and somehow broken through the gate (which they certainly would not have done). The few mercenaries hired by Lord Famm would have been sufficient to fight off the attack and drive the land-toilers back to the village. Then, when word had been sent south to the neighboring lords (whose own land-toilers were very much like the land-toilers of Scoms) a coordinated attack would have spelled the final defeat of the land-toilers. Then would begin the trials and retribution, the hangings, the return to the old balance of things, and the obscuring of memory. The children would be told by survivors in the village of how the foolish men who rose up were killed, how the village was burned, how the Lord Famm walked the cowed mass in his bright armor and blue flesh, and how the words of the priests extolled the virtues of obedience, honor, and subservience to the rightful way of things. That was all how things would have happened, and that is what the priest would have said, except that he had been turned into a giant, and he had led the charge on the fort, and he had seen the truth. He saw the visions even now.

The Witness pushed one swordsman down, and as that man stood up the Witness buried the hammer in his chest. The blow that flung him backward again, into the wall, and left him crumpled at its foot. A villager crept up to the still man, slipped the unused sword from his hand, and offered it to The Witness, who did not want it. He would have said so, but he could not think of the words. He just shook his head and held up the hammer, which was dark with blood. Then he looked out across the inner yard of the fort, and he saw that the dozen swordsmen were indeed holding his villagers at bay, and that the nearest of the fort's inner buildings was already on fire -- it looked to be the barracks -- and he saw that the day was clear and the air was light and the hammer seemed alive in his hand.

He sickened at the sight of the dead and the wounded, the hacked limbs, the bloodied faces, the brains that leaked from the head of a man whose family still waited in the village, the guts that spilled from another pale villager who lay still alive and weeping at the feet of one of Famm's swordsmen. He saw the blood on his own hammer, and these sights combined to fill his throat with what seemed a choking sensation, a need to cough up the bile of death and horror. But as it traveled up his throat and took shape, as it became a *cry*, he let himself become lost. He staggered, and a roar poured out him ragged and soaring, capturing all who heard it. All the men in the fort turned to look at him, and he held up the hammer high, for all to see, and he wound up the cry with a sense of power that seemed to flow from him like a river. Like the mighty Prava, life-giving and unstoppable.

The Witness leaped at the nearest of Famm's swordsmen, who had felled three of the villagers himself, and he seized the man by the arm in which he held his bloody sword. This he snapped with little effort. The Witness then smashed his head in with the hammer. He then flung the body up into the air and his own strength astonished him. He had no fear now, and leaped to the foot of the steps that ran up to the parapet. Here he brained another swordsman who faltered before him, and this one too he flung into the air like a clump of dirt. He shouted in triumph, exultant, his hammer held up high overhead, and his men came alive. They fought like demons now. Famm's confused men now tried to run. They came down in a swarm of knives and clubs, their own stolen swords, and angry grasping hands.

A sharp pain exploded in the Witness's back. He reached around to feel the shaft of an arrow protruding from him. He turned around on the steps and saw that up on the parapet, hiding at the very end and notching another arrow into his bow, was a young man whose hair was long and blonde, and who tried to hide himself behind a wooden plank. The Witness called out to him. "Boy! Come here. Give me the bow!"

The archer aimed straight at the Witness. He pulled the arrow back hard against the string and the bow bent to his strength.

The Witness climbed the steps. The hammer shimmered in his hand, the pain in his back burned.

"Put it down boy," The Witness said. "Do not die today. Not like this. You can join us! Be one of us! The Wood needs you! Let the land breathe you in, let it be your blood and your soul! Do like I have done!"

The boy loosed the arrow. It buried itself in The Witness's chest, and The Witness nearly fell backward with surprise and shock. The boy's nervousness became a mad laughter, and he clambered up onto the dirty grey wall, away from the Witness, who looked down at the arrow and leaned back against the wall. His men, who had been watching from the yard, now streamed up the steps toward where he stood. They had killed Famm's men, and the barracks building was in flames, and the horses in the stable were rioting with fear. The dead were twenty or more, and their blood leaked into the soil.

The boy danced along the top of the wall, but he saw immediately that the parapet on the other side of the gate had already fallen to the angry villagers, who started to jeer him. They stepped up onto the wall themselves, with swords, and down below waited others, who picked up rocks and threw them at the boy. His terror quickly became overwhelming. He ran back along the wall toward the Witness, then stopped and looked behind him, where two villagers with clubs now trailed precariously a few steps behind. Rocks flew past him from below, then hit him. Once, glancingly, then a second one solidly. He threw up his arms, crying out, and a foot slipped out from under him. He toppled backward off the wall, shrieking as he went. The villagers came after him, and the Witness did not see how they killed him. His cries ended quickly, and a cheer went up from below.

The Witness's strength seemed an endless reservoir. He put his hand on the arrow shaft, which protruded from his chest below his neck, and he began to slowly twist it back and forth. The pain rose and fell with his twists, but he bore it silently. He felt a sharp jab, then a another, and he winced as he pulled the arrow whole from his body. Blood poured from the wound, but he did not care. He snapped the arrow in half and threw it down. His men cheered again, and he descended the steps from the parapet. Waving his hammer over his head, he ran to the main house, and his men followed with their torches and their new swords. They stormed into the house, into the long dark corridors of the ancient place, and they ripped the furnishings from the rooms, the tapestries from the cold stone walls, and smashed everything that was peaceful and decorative.

Then shouts came from the courtyard. *Come Witness*, they cried. *Look what we have done*!

*   *   *

The villagers had captured Famm and his family in the courtyard as they tried to flee. The wagon had come speeding from a hidden place within the fort, and one man (who now stood proudly aside) had leapt into it and attacked the driver, who was Lord Famm himself. They had overturned the wagon only after the capture, in a show of enthusiasm. A dozen men excitedly recounted the story to The Witness.

Lady Famm held her children close to her, all crying and fearful beside the overturned wagon. Her long white hair tressed carefully, her blue face rigid as she begged for their lives. Villagers worked to cut the horses free. The Lord Famm himself lay dying in the dirt, clutching at his guts. His blue face bruised and beaten. Villagers lurked near him. Ready to finish him off.

"What are you, giant?" Famm asked. "Why have you come here? Why have you chosen me?"

"I was a priest, Famm. You remember. I was *your* priest. Then I went into the forest and the spirits found me. They showed me the truth, the past, what is real and remains so. I saw it! I have been made holy, and turned into a warrior to free Thane."

Famm studied him coldly.

"No, Tare, you have not been made holy. You have fallen under the sway of the demon. You are deranged, and the heretics of the village follow you as they would any giant. There is a God you know. The demon might cloud out God's light briefly, but it cannot make God cease to be."

The Witness did not intervene as the villagers killed him. He ordered that the family be held in safety. They might make good hostages, he thought.

* * *

The wailing of the villagers did not cease. When the fires in the village were finally put out and the dead collected, they wept. They cleaned the wounds of those who survived the battle, and they wept still for the dead. The Witness's heart was with them, but he could not share their sorrow. All those who died would join the Wood, and all the pain in the world would be erased for them. But for the living, the sons and daughters who stood in tears beside their mothers' knees, the women whose lives were cast forever into the dust, the parents whose sons now lay lifeless among the heroes, there could be no erasure. They looked to the Witness for hope on this black day, and he offered them the vision. He told them of the visions, the transformation, the call of the Wood, and his own faith.

"There are no more Masters!" He told them. "Free people do not have masters! There are only Devils! And I will not rest until they are gone! In this hour we must consign our friends to memory, to the Wheel, to the spirits of the forest, and we must take solace in those things. The Old Belief came down to us from the beginning of time. We can feel the power of the Wood growing again, restoring again! We must spread the word now. We must go to the villages, to the farms, to the castles of the traitor lords! We must go with fire and sword! Drive the Devils and their slaves out of the land! Destroy the false church that calls itself True! Freedom! Faith! I promise! Who will follow?"

They cheered him there, at the foot of Famm's hill. The manor house burned behind him. The people of Scoms cheered their leader, the giant, and they saw the future with him. He held his hammer high.

Chapter Nine: The Call

They came from the forest and the outlying villages. They came with their own clubs and spears, their own knives. They came with the weapons and gold of their masters, the small landholders whose stronghold might be a single round tower overlooking a single poor village in a deep and remote valley. These men and their families were cut down in the night, by surprise, and left to rot. Their villagers left immediately, abandoning the shacks and huts to which they had been consigned, and going out across the land.

To the free village.

The giant prayed in the empty remains of the old fort, and his prayer sent the call out across the land to the acolytes of the living Wood, the Old Believers. They whispered in their hidden dens, in moments where they did not fear, that a new fire had come into the land. In many places the Old Believers rose immediately and came at the enemy with knives. In others they whispered and prayed, and they kept the news among themselves. They walked in darkness, under the dominion of the traitor lords and the false church, and behind everything was the laughing blue face of the overlord. Should there slip any sign that they were loyal to the Old Belief, to the old lords, they would burn in the village square while their cowed friends and allies watched from behind the line of pikemen. The Witness knew this. In holy visions he saw the faces of the Old Believers who awaited him in places where the enemy was strong, he saw their silent loyalty. The visions came in dreams, and his prayers sent out the call.

From the free village.

He had been touched by the Wood, by the spirits of the forest, and the land-toilers knew this to look at him. The villagers of Scoms were the first to pledge themselves to him, and he gathered the young men around him and they took up the weapons from the fort and the dead. They took up swords and spears, arrows and axes, and their courage was unquestionable. They watched the approaches to the village, and talked bravely of how they would fight the armies of all the great dukes and lords. The Witness laughed with them and drank wine from the stores of Lord Famm, and he held counsel with the elders of the village. They blessed him and his enterprise, and they said that they had seen him in their dreams long before the transformation. They revealed that the whole village had been loyal to the Old Belief even during his tenure as a priest of the false church, and he was amused by this. It did not disturb him to see through the veil of lies. It was part of his enlightenment. He walked among his new friends and rejoiced in true company. They buried the bodies of the dead according to the old way, consecrated in tribute to the Wood, and the Witness led them in a dance of the Wheel, and the women were in one circle with their hands interlocking, and the men were in another, and outside of that circle was another and another and another. They had eight circles of people, all rotating within one another, and all sang the old chant while a hubstone pyre lit up the night. The Witness stood at the center of the wheel, drunk with wine, singing and waving his hands with the song, and the singers were suddenly possessed by the spirits of the forest. All their voices rose to a single sustained note, the rotations of the Wheel became more intense, more hurried, and then the Witness floated up into the air, high off the ground, and the rest of the dancers and singers also floated up. They spun their of their own accord, high above the bloody earth and the buried remains of their men, and their joy was unencumbered by the world. Wheels turned within wheels, filling the sky, and at the hub of all of them was the Witness. He sang and sang the song of the world, and the night seemed to last forever.

In the free village.

*   *   *

The children followed the giant Witness wherever he went. He came down from the empty ruins of Famm's fort alone. He had prayed through the night, and his prayers had been like waves in a still pond, radiating outward to the silent fish who waited beneath the water, who had waited forever for the first stone to fall from the sky. He had prayed in the ashes of the manor house, in a Wheel that he had built from the rocks of the house itself. He had kneeled and prayed all through the night. For wisdom, that he might know how to lead his people. For courage, that he might lead again in battle, and that his men might follow. For vision, that he could see the end of this enterprise, that he could understand the final shape of the world after his remaking of it.

The children awaited him at the foot of the hill. They looked on him with fascination and fear at his size, which was far greater than any other man. There was a dirty-faced boy and girls whose long hair was matted and stringy. They smiled shyly at him, and he stood there for a while to look out at the land. The long fields, the village in the distance beneath its stand of trees, the long columns of cooking-fire smoke, the far line where the forest took up, and the green hills and mountains.

Where would he lead his people next? To the south and southwest lay the dominion of the Lord Sabodisho, whose own cruel hands begged cutting, and whose own villages would rise as soon as the Witness's men came to them. He knew this already, by the whisper of the forest spirits. He had heard the whisper in the night, lost in a long musical tone, emanating like his own soul.

To the east lay the poorer lands of Lord Bruns Bramlett, whose raiders went often into the northern lands, the mountain range that loomed in the north, and who would be a cruel opponent. The Witness envisioned the tree-limb on which he would string the man up to die.

To the north lay only the mountains, and the hills and valleys that came before them. There was no Thanian lord there, and the mountain people were lawless and cruel themselves. The Witness had not seen an attack in his brief tenure as priest of Scoms, but he had heard of them. The secret attacks in the dead of night, the kidnapping of women and children, the trading of slaves among the chieftains of the mountains. He had heard all the tales, and he knew that Bruns Bramlett had just recently taken to warring again with the mountain people.

The Witness was deep in thought as he passed the long encampment of those who had come to follow him. They waved and cheered, and their dirty faces were hopeful and young. They gathered around fires and awaited the Witness's command. There was nothing to say yet. He waved at them as he passed, but he had no words or inspirations to give them. He had only the visions, the prayers, the strength of one hundred men. The day was long and bright, and he went down into the forest. The children left him alone at the forest's edge, and he was not ever at peace.

The Witness met with the elders of Scoms and the surrounding villages. These were old men and women whose true roles had been hidden from him while he had been their priest. They gathered together around a lonely fire, and they wrapped themselves in shawls and robes to keep out the chill of the morning air. The Witness came down into their glade and sat with them. He was not cold, and the morning air felt like nothing to him.

"The lords will come, Witness. They will bring an army to destroy us. Our people have followed you, they have made themselves known. This is the worst mistake. We have struggled to remain hidden from the lords. We have kept our people silent, our ways secretive, our souls unseen behind opaque eyes. The lords have mistaken our strategy for their own success. You know that."

"Yes," The Witness said. He himself had thought the heresy largely routed from this place.

"What will you do? Lead them into the mountains? Where will you go? The secret of Famm's demise will only last a little longer. It cannot go on. When Sabodisho finds out, he will sound the alarm. Or perhaps it will be Bruns Bramlett. Or perhaps an envoy from Visselno, who comes with word for Famm and finds the fort in ruins. How can we ensure that the single rider will not be our undoing?"

The Witness sat quietly and listened as the others debated the danger, the threat. He sat in the shady glen, in the warmth of the fire, and he let the words of the elders flit about him. He could not think how to address their concerns, their worries, with reason and logic that they would understand. They were the product of the old way, the quiet and hidden way that the Old Believers undertook when they were weak and the night was their only shield. He knew in his heart that those days were now just a memory.

"I will free all the land," The Witness said finally. "I will see the Devils driven from Thane and the traitor lords with them. I will cleanse this land."

"How?" said the old woman who was called the Widow. She sat in the center of the group of elders, and her face was haunted and ancient. She had seen the past too, The Witness knew as he looked at her. Her useless eyes seemed to stare at cross-purposes, but she craned her head toward him. "Tell us how you will free the land when you have at your disposal only the tired and poor land-toilers. Tell us how you will capture all the land between the rivers, how you will storm the forts of the lords, how you will take Visselno and Mesto-on-Leva, how you will besiege Riadom and last out the winter outside its great walls while the Devils come from across the plains to relieve the city. Tell us this! I want to hear your plan."

The Witness tried to speak, began to formulate words, but realized that he could not answer the questions. He could *see*, but he could not articulate. He saw in his heart that he could make the land free with fire and blood, that he could be the hand of the Wood, that his visions were real. He could explain nothing.

"Tell us!" Cried the Widow as the Witness stood up. He walked to the edge of the glen and stopped. Then he said, "What I have in my heart is straight from the Wood. What I see is straight from the Wood. I cannot tell you why or how, I only know that the truth is in me. I say that I will free the land. The Wood has told me to go ahead. Look at me! I am a warrior now. *The Wood has made me that*!"

She called after him but he did not turn around or stop. He left the woods with his hammer and his faith, and he went to the men who had come to follow him. He raised the hammer before them, and they did not ask for confirmation. They saw, they knew. And he himself only saw and knew. It was called faith. The Wood had made *him* a warrior. He could not explain why.

*   *   *

The Witness set out before dawn with his brothers behind him. They were the poor and the lost, and their families they left behind. They left behind also the cooking fires and animals, and the homes that all had known. They set out along the path they wound through the woods to the estate of Lord Sabodisho, whose land encompassed a dozen villages. The Witness and his men would show Sabodisho the harvest of what he had sown: blood and fear.

The older men had craggy faces and rough hands, the leathery complexion of long years under the sun, and the pitiless eyes of laborers. They bore their weapons like they were holy objects, and this seemed right to the Witness. The holy war would now begin. They were the tools of the servants of God, of the spirits of the wood. The younger men walked proudly. Their faces shined when they held their weapons, their excitement was like a spirit itself, illuminating and energizing, turning their focus together to the single goal of freedom. The Witness harnessed that spirit and the young marched with him. He would not deny any man a chance to strike a blow for freedom.

He led them through the clear morning air on that bright day, when the year Zero approached to within shouting distance and the end of the old world had already begun. He waved the hammer high when they came to the edge of Sabodisho's lands, where the trees broke and the fields were filled with land-toilers. The Witness raised his hammer and called out to his men:

"For Thane!"

At village after village they joined him. Their seers had seen him in visions.

* * *

He recalled much later how they stormed the fort of Sabodisho. How their spies had opened the gates. How like a dream it was as he entered the yard of the enemy. Then the world of thought and rationality faded away and he saw only long images, spectres that danced before him with a sense of vague threat, and just as quickly vanished. He felt drunk with power and rage, and the faces that he saw he smashed with the hammer. They were young and old, men with swords and with other undefinable objects in their hands. He smashed everything that he could find, drunk with rage, a killer with the strength of a hundred men. He cried out "Thane! Thane! Thane!" as he killed, and no wound seemed real, no opponent too quick.

Soon the yard was still. The Witness stood alone in the center of an open space, and his hands with slick and hot with the blood of the dead who lay around him. Their brains and skulls were smashed and beaten in. Their arms were snapped off, their faces still twisted in fearful cries.

The land-toilers stood at the gate, staring in at the giant, who now hung his head and stared at the dead.

Chapter Ten: Shame

She had lost her soul to the repository of dreams. How many nights had she gazed into the future, the past? She had seen great spirals in the mountains, the grey ancient ones who still walked the high places, who drifted in the snowy clouds that hid the peaks from view. These were peaks that she had seen only in her sleep, when her soul traveled far from the island, far from the day and her sorry state. She was nothing to her family, just the last of the girl children, and the even the day itself was not her friend. She was lost in its light, blinded and tense, free only when sleep took her and the miracle of flight was hers.

Petra, daughter of the Lord Harkess, walked alone on the ridge that led north from the Monastery. She followed a trail that wound between heavy grey rocks that protruded from the grass on the treeless ridge, along the edge of the sea-cliff. She wrapped her black cloak tightly around her to keep out the salty winds that gusted up from the cliff, the cold winds of the northern sea, and she shielded her face with one hand. Her skin was pale, her eyes deep and black, and her mouth was closed tight in a slit that could not let forth a smile. So close to the sad soul of the earth had she come that no happiness seemed real to her, no joy was more than a shallow instant, an odd breath got while drowning.

Clouds filled the grey sky above her, and she did not look back at the great wall of the world that rose up to fill the sky behind her. Soon it would cast its shadow on the island, and her world would become ice and darkness again. Then she would sleep and dream without the interventions of her father, who knew nothing, or her mother, who lived only in the moment.

"You were born to commune with the Wood," her mother told her once. "If we were still in Thane you would have become its priestess. But you must be dutiful now, and on this island you can never be that."

Shame, shame, shame. This was all she felt. They wanted her to marry, to have a child. A son, that is. To replace her lost brother, to lead the people of the island, to assure that they would not disappear into the mists of what has been lost to memory. She could not do it. The feeling of a man's hand on her body provoked only more shame, and she had stood on these same cliffs entranced by the only prospect that made her heart flutter. This was death, the vampire, the seducer. She knew that one day she would succumb to the whisper of relief, the promise of an end to the days, to the pain, to the thing that was *Petra*.

She hated herself. She would murder herself one day. She had seen it in her dreams.

Before she realized it, she had reached her destination. She had walked the whole length of the ridge deep in thought, and now stood before the dark stone tower that her grandfather had built with his own hands. This was her secret place, far from the meddling eyes of the Monastery or the villages. She had always come here to escape them, drifting for long hours in the world of dreams, looking out through the only window. This faced away from the world and out to the open sea. This was where her grandfather had sat too, his back to the world and to the Monastery, embittered and mad, before the chill got into his bones and carried him away to the world of the dead. Petra looked around her, at the rocky treeless ridge, the grey skies. She imagined that the world of the dead was very much like this place: separated from the world of the living by an insurmountable wall, still and full of spite, full of fear.

She walked around to the front of the tower. Inscribed just above the arched entrance were the words *Heart's Ease*. This was her Mericet's name for the place. It had been his Heart's Ease, with his back to the world, looking out into the dark and cold sea of infinity.

The tower rose up sharply from its place at the tip of the island. Waves crashed at the bottom of the cliffs, and winds gusted violently around Petra as she slipped into the narrow entrance beneath the inscription, into the shadowy passage within the tower. Immediately inside the tower the narrow passage became wider, and Petra stood in a dark stone room. There was nothing in this place. The wind whipped through it, and Petra went to the foot of the stairs, which were almost indiscernible in the half-light. She climbed the stairs, which were narrow and cold, and which wound around inside the tower three times as they ascended. This was all in near darkness. She felt the places along the walls where torches might have been placed in her grandfather's day. There was nothing there now.

At the top of the stairs Petra came out into a confined, circular room. It was as empty as her life. A single portal looked out to the open sea. To the north, where there was nothing.

She sat down against the wall, beside the open portal, in the same spot where she always sat. She rested her head against a curved stone that was not uncomfortable, and curled her legs up beneath her heavy cloak. She wrapped it closer against her, and shifted herself until her body rested effortlessly against the wall. In the empty room.

This was her sleeping place. Her place of flying.

Soon she was drowsy.

Good, she thought. *Let me discover!*

Then she slept.

www.ingramcontent.com/pod-product-compliance
Ingram Content Group UK Ltd.
Pitfield, Milton Keynes, MK11 3LW, UK
UKHW041434180426
11947UKWH00007B/442